A New Direction

Alexander Martin

Published by Alexander Martin, 2024.

This is a work of fiction. Similarities to real people, places, or events are entirely coincidental.

A NEW DIRECTION

First edition. April 14, 2024.

Copyright © 2024 Alexander Martin.

ISBN: 979-8224799664

Written by Alexander Martin.

Table of Contents

A New Direction

By: Alexander Martin

Copyright 2023 Alexander Martin

Author Note:

This is a work of fiction, none of the characters are real or are they based on real people or events. Please do not take the actions or expressions noted in this story as the Author's outlook on life or respected behavior of anybody alive or deceased.

All characters in this story are over the age of Eighteen.

Please have fun and enjoy reading these stories.

Chapter One: Trouble in Paradise

Tony banged on the bathroom door as I emptied my stomach for the third time.

"Are you okay?" he asked.

"Go away!" I yelled as I kneeled over the toilet. "I don't want to talk to you!"

"We can talk about this," Tony said, banging on the door again and trying to turn the handle. "You know I can break the door down."

Tony was my husband, and he had been a firefighter in his prime. Now he was a decorated and respected investigator.

"Do you want me to break the door?"

I wiped my mouth and stood up. "I am coming out," I nodded. I washed my mouth and opened the door pushing past Tony's sizeable muscular frame.

"All I want to do is talk," Tony said as he sat on the bed.

"I need to drink," I replied as I walked into the living room.

"They overcharge for...." Before I opened one of the tiny liquor bottles in the hotel's small refrigerator, Tony started to say.

"Go ahead, talk," I said as I picked up another.

We were in the mountains. This hotel was our favorite spot to get away, especially for the holidays. We had come up two days before our kids would arrive.

I say kids lightly, as the two were well past their childhood years. Katy was going on nineteen, and Dawson was going to be twenty-four. Katy was entering college while Dawson was in his last year.

Frederick, my oldest, was in the military and wouldn't be joining us this year.

I half-listened to my husband as he tried to explain himself. I drank the last of the tiny bottles as he droned on. What he didn't realize was that I was ready to puke again.

We had come up early because we wanted to rekindle a spark in our marriage, especially in the bedroom.

I didn't expect him to admit that he had been regularly jerking himself off to porn. I wasn't surprised about the porn as he was a man, and I had brought myself to a few late-night self-induced orgasms through a few porn videos.

What I didn't expect was the type of porn. Cuckold porn. Tony had saved hundreds of videos of men sitting in the corner watching their wives get fucked by other men. Tony revealed that he was interested in this for us.

At first, I watched just to see what the big deal was; maybe if I watched, I would find out why my husband wanted to fuck other men's wives as their husbands watched him.

Then it dawned on me as his dick formed a tent in his tight bed pants. He didn't want to be the man doing the fucking. He wanted to be the man in the corner.

When he told me he had a few guys in mind that would love to fuck me, I made a beeline for the bathroom. I couldn't imagine fucking another man with Tony sitting in the corner, jerking himself off.

"So, that's why I think...." Tony said as he looked at me. "You haven't heard a word I said, have you?"

"No," I shook my head. "I am your wife, yours!" I yelled at him. "I said, I do to you, not to some other guys!"

"And you would still be my wife," Tony sighed. "You asked me what my interests were, did you want me to lie to you?"

"Interests," I said as I looked at him. "Not your..." I stopped myself as I didn't want to call my husband a sick, perverted half-human. What kind of husbands would like to sit and watch multiple men use their wives?

"You were going to call me a Beta, weren't you?" Tony laughed as he got up. "Just like your brother when he found out about our son."

"You leave Dawson out of this conversation!" I said, standing up.

Dawson had come out of the closet in his first year of college, letting us know he was gay and had been dating guys for many years.

My brother had called him a Beta and other names, and I struck him hard. That was the last time my brother and I talked or saw each other.

"No," I shook my head. "I wouldn't call you that," I said, looking at Tony. No one would call Tony that, not to his face anyway.

"I am sure you were thinking it, though," Tony smiled. "Just like those retards that hang out in the forums calling other people names behind fake names and using anonymous profiles."

"I am nothing like them," I said, walking past him and into the bedroom. "If I wanted to call you that, I would, and you know it!"

I couldn't stand the keyboard heroes online thinking their opinion mattered in the grand scheme.

As someone that worked in the medical profession as a psychologist, it was all I heard about someone getting their jollies off by knocking someone else down. When confronted in real life, most fell like a ton of bricks. I should know I had faced a lot of them.

"So," Tony said.

"So, what," I asked. "If you are asking if it is something I would consider, I think you know the answer."

"Just like that?" Tony asked as he stood in the doorway. "What if I had asked you for another female to join?"

"Now," I said, shaking my head. He knew I had experimented in college and hadn't liked the experience. I had thought about it.

"Oh, now here comes the hypocrisy," Tony said. "Everyone thinks it's okay to have a threesome with two women and a guy, but...."

"No," I said, cutting him off. "A threesome is when all participants are involved, if you said you would be participating along with the other man, I would think about it. But you would not be participating. You will be just sitting there with your dick in your hand."

"What's the difference?" Tony asked.

I couldn't believe he was trying to justify his sick fantasy. "I will not be fucked by someone else while you watch, that's final!"

"Fine!" Tony slammed the door to the bedroom.

Then I heard the door to our room slam. I was sure he was going to one of the rooms we had booked for the kids.

I let out a scream and then plummeted backward into the bed.

KATY AND HER BOYFRIEND Mike were the first to arrive. They had flown in from Arizona. Tony hated Mike as he was one of those women come first types what the internet trolls would call a simp.

Even now, he was carrying Katy's bags and her purse. Katy wore the pants, shoes, and all the other clothes in their relationship, and all Mike did was say yes.

"Mike," Tony said as he looked at the bright red purse hanging off Mike's shoulder.

"Hey sir," Mike said as he held out his hand.

"Lose the purse," Tony said as he looked down at Mike.

"Dad!" Katy said as she took the purse away from her boyfriend.

"One day," Tony said as he hugged our daughter. "I am going to take him hunting, and he will return a changed man."

"I doubt that," I said as I looked at Tony.

I was sure as Metrosexual as Mike was, I doubt he would let someone else sleep with Katy while he watched. I had seen Mike get angry. Under all that gloss and spiky hair gel was a scary man.

"I love your nails, Janice," Mike said as he held my hands.

"Thought you would, but no, I am not telling you where I got them done."

"Such a pain," Mike laughed as he hugged me.

Dawson and his boyfriend Craig met us at the ski lift as we prepared for the mountain's most challenging course. They had come up later and were already geared for the slopes.

"Where's the other?" I asked as I saw them heading for us.

"Over there," Craig said as he pointed to a tall black male.

They had brought up one of their friends, who had nowhere to go for the holidays. Craig was tall and muscular, just like Tony. In contrast, Dawson was skin and bones. Their friend, on the other hand, towered over everybody. I guessed he was at least seven feet tall or more.

"Gregg meet the family," Dawson said as he introduced us.

"You must play basketball," Tony said, looking at Gregg.

Gregg wasn't just tall. He was very built and attractive. I had found a few black males attractive before I got married, but I never acted on it. Sometimes I wondered about it.

"You would think, right?" Craig answered. "No, our boy Gregg here is a big softy!"

"Keep calling me that, and I will make you a short softy!" Gregg smiled.

When Dawson first introduced Craig to the family, Tony tried to pull that macho bullshit, the man of the house crap, but Craig had none of it. Since then, Tony knew he had to choose his words. Now I wanted to blurt out his big secret and see how they all took it.

"We going to go skiing or just stand here?" Katy asked, staring at us. She was just like her mother, never holding back her thoughts.

"I have never skied," Gregg said, staring at all of us.

"Well, this course isn't for you," I said as I looked down the steep hill.

I saw one of the instructors that had taught us in the past. "Tim!" I waved.

Tim was the best on the mountain. "We got a rookie in our midst; can you take him to the beginners?" I asked.

"Sure," Tim said as he looked at all of us. He knew the whole family as we came here every year. "You must be the rookie," he said as he looked at Gregg.

"That would be me," Gregg laughed.

"Come on," Tim nodded. "I will get you going in no time."

"YOU CHEATED!" KATY said as she punched Craig's shoulder.

"I didn't see a rule that said don't cut people off," Craig laughed as he pushed her.

The two of them acted like Frederick and her when they got together. In a way, Craig had become another brother to Katy. Craig and Mike also hit it off, even though Craig sometimes went overboard, making fun of Mike's hair.

"Well, for the third year in a row, I am the champion," I said as we sat at the large picnic table. Our skis were put up, and snow boots were on.

"I knew it," Mike said, nodding his head.

"Knew what?" I asked.

"Gingers don't have a soul," Mike laughed.

The others joined him, including Tony. "Ha-ha!" I smiled at him. "Not my fault you all suck!"

"Here they you are," Tim said as he approached our picnic table. "Rookie is no longer a rookie anymore. My job is complete."

"You're the best, Tim!" Katy said.

"Well, on skis, he isn't," Tim shrugged. "Just can't get the balance right," Tim said, patting Gregg. "But on this," Tim said, holding up a snowboard. "The boy's got some skills!"

"No, shit?" Craig asked.

"Show them," Tim said as he looked at Gregg.

Gregg put his phone onto the table and pressed play. Sure enough, the tall man was shredding the snow on the snowboard. He even pulled off a few tricks.

"Well, call me a fool," Craig said as he looked at the video.

"Fool!" Katy said quickly.

"You walked into that one," I laughed. "Thanks again, Tim!"

Tim left us and went on his way.

Gregg came with us on the intermediate course. He kept up with us the whole way on his snowboard. He even pulled ahead of me at one point. I had to pull out an old trick to gain my advantage and pull out the win.

"Mom!" Katy said as she finished last again.

"What?" I asked innocently.

"You booty bumped Gregg out the way!" Tony said with a smile.

I had forgotten about last night while I looked at him for a while. Then when I saw him standing next to Gregg and envisioned one of the videos of a black male ejaculating inside one of the women and the husband licking her out afterward, it came crashing down onto me.

"All is fair in racing, right?" Gregg said. "Including using the occasional booty bump."

"Yeah," I said as I pulled off my gloves.

"You, okay?" Dawson asked as he approached me.

I wanted to tell them. I wanted to tell them what I had found out and why I wasn't the usual life of the party self.

"Just tired," I lied. "You guys carry on. You should show Gregg the halfpipe. I am sure he will like it."

"Okay," Mike said, "If you are sure that...."

"Yeah," I said as all my boys surrounded me. "I am good, trust me."

"Okay," Craig said. "Give us a call, if anything."

"Absolutely," I nodded as they all took off for the halfpipe.

"You just can't...." Tony said as he looked at me.

"Shut up!" I said, shaking my head and ensuring they were out of earshot range. "I just need time Tony, let me have it, then maybe we can talk."

"If that's the way you want it," Tony said as he skated off. "You should call your brother and apologize; you are just as close-minded as him. If you can't accept it then we need to go our separate ways after this holiday."

"Are you serious?" I asked, looking at the kids laughing and joking with each other on their way to the half pipe.

"I will not be looked down upon," Tony said. "And if you can't accept what I like, then so be it. Make your choice!"

"Right now?" I asked, staring up at the man I had married. "You're putting me into a corner right now?"

"Yes, if you love me, you will accept it, unconditionally," Tony shrugged. "If you can't."

"What? You will find someone that will?" I shook my head. "Is that what you were going to say?"

"Maybe," Tony stared down at me. "So, what will it be Cynthia?"

"Fuck off!" I said as I skated towards the hotel.

I LAY IN BED FOR WHAT seemed like hours. I had never told my husband to fuck off. Was he right that I was just as close-minded to his newfound interest as my brother was to the idea of two people of the same sex being in love?

I knew one person I could talk to, and they would give me their opinion.

"Hey son," I said via my satellite phone.

"Mom," Frederick answered. Frederick was my oldest child and the most open-minded person that I knew. He saw through everyone's shit like a human emotion detector. "What did Dad do this time?"

"I hate it when you do that," I laughed.

I told him about our argument. And for the first time, I saw a bit of anger flare on his face. Frederick was easygoing and level-headed. It took a lot to get him angry.

"You're going to leave him, aren't you?" Frederick asked.

"Thinking about it," I answered.

"You should," Frederick said. "Not because of his interest, but making you feel that you are wrong. As well as many other things."

"So, I am not?" I asked.

"You both are," Frederick said. "But he shouldn't throw it in your face and especially slam you into a corner like that; he had time to process this new interest. Knowing Dad, he probably read articles and searched the internet about it. You've only had a few hours to process it. Given the right time, I am sure you might understand it better."

I nodded. As always, Frederick was right. If Tony hadn't pushed it, maybe I wouldn't have yelled. "Thanks," I said as I saw another person behind him.

"Got to go," Frederick said. "Call you in two days?"

"Absolutely," I waved.

The timing was perfect as the door opened, and everyone came crashing in. "Mom, Gregg won a contest!" Katy yelled as she ran towards me and jumped onto the couch.

"Yeah, he pulled off some trick at the end, that put him in second place," Mike said. "You should have seen it."

"Congrats," I nodded.

"Yeah, no one to booty bump me out of the way this time," Gregg said as he sat at the bar.

"Oh," Dawson said as he shook his head. "Low blow!"

"You know this family takes our contest seriously, right?" I smiled.

Gregg took his glove and threw it down in front of the couch.

"Well?" Gregg said.

"Your friend has spunk," I nodded. "You do know I grew up on these mountains, right?"

"I hear a whole lot of talking," Gregg laughed.

"Tomorrow, my course, my rules?" I said, standing up and looking at him.

"Time?" Gregg said as he stood up and looked down at me.

"Noon," I smiled. "No one wants to wake up early."

"True!" Gregg said.

Everyone laughed, and we sat back down.

BEFORE MY BIG CHALLENGE, I went shopping with Mike, Katy, and Craig. I wanted to get Gregg some presents since no one had bought him anything yet. I didn't want him to feel left out when we opened ours.

Craig was a big help as he had known him the longest. Soon, we had enough presents wrapped and under the tree before the distraction team brought Gregg back to the hotel.

"READY?" I ASKED.

"Sure," Gregg nodded.

We went on a professional course. It was a mixture of intermediate and experienced. It was my favorite because I knew it like the back of my hand.

"Rules," Gregg asked as he stomped his feet into a newly bought snowboard. The distraction team had taken him to the ski shop a few miles from the hotel.

I stood next to him in my usual white snow gear. "Easy, since you're the challenger, you give me a ten-second lead, if you finish before me you win, finish more than ten seconds after me, you lose."

"What do I get when I win?" Gregg said as he stared at me with a grin as he lowered his goggles over his eyes.

Was he flirting with me? I could see he was eyeing my ass as he lowered his goggles. Excellent two can play that game.

"Let's make it interesting," I said, getting close to him so no one could hear. "Loser, does whatever the winner wants until Christmas morning?"

"Whatever?" Gregg grinned. Again, I could see his eyes staring right at me.

Shit, my plan backfired. I was sure he was going to call my bluff. The bastard was flirting with me, and now I just teased back.

"I will hold you to that," Gregg said as he got ready.

"You two racing or talking?" Tony asked.

Tim nodded to us as he held out the flare. He fired it into the air, and I took off. I counted to ten inside my head and looked back.

"Shit!" I said as I saw Gregg rocketing down the hill.

I had the lead as I turned the corner, there was a medium jump ahead, and I hit it fast. Soaring through the air before landing, I had time to look back for a second.

"Fuck me!" I said as Gregg hit the jump. "Damn, he is fast," I said as I rounded the third corner, taking it as quickly and low as possible.

I looked back and didn't see him. Maybe he fell. I didn't hear a bell or the siren that indicated an injury on the course.

I sped up just in case. I went over the bumps. I was getting close to the finish line when I heard a thud from behind.

"Mother fucker!" I cursed.

Gregg had taken the shortcut, meaning he jumped and landed the big jump. He was right beside me.

"So, I was thinking," Gregg said. "We should go out for dinner."

"You haven't...." I said before Gregg booty bumped me into the wall as we turned the last corner.

Everyone cheered as Gregg crossed the line.

"Shit!" I said as I slowly crossed the line.

"YOU CHEATED," I SAID as I secretly met Gregg later that night. It wasn't easy getting away from everybody.

"Just returning the favor," Gregg said as we caught a taxi.

My heart was racing. I didn't know why, but I found the experience thrilling. Here I was, a married woman with another man about to go out on a date. I could count all the males I had ever been on a date with on one hand. Tony was number five.

"You look great, by the way," Gregg said.

"You don't look so bad yourself," I replied.

He looked handsome in his tight shirt and black jeans. I didn't think of putting anything too fancy on, as I would have tipped everyone off.

We had a great night at a restaurant near the hotel. It was one of the best nights I had had in a long time. We talked for hours about everything and anything. I caught him staring at my chest even though it was covered up.

I saw him sneaking and stealing glances plenty of times over the table. I didn't mind. It was something I had gotten accustomed to when I was around men. Having a large chest was something that ran in the family.

"So, what now?" Gregg asked as we caught a taxi back to the hotel.

"The date is over," I shrugged, genuinely disappointed.

"Well, it isn't Christmas morning officially," Gregg said as he looked at the clock.

"Four minutes," I said as I looked at my watch.

"So, the rules still apply," Gregg said.

"Yes, they do," I answered.

We got out of the taxi and stood outside the hotel. I looked up at the large hotel at the rows of windows and balconies that went up to the top. A few floors up were my husband and my family, a few floors down, and I was standing outside the hotel with a young man and butterflies in my stomach.

"Kiss me," Gregg said.

I stood still for a moment; part of me wanted to tell him no, and the other part wanted to kiss him. The other part won. I tiptoed and kissed him. He held me tight and grabbed my ass, pulling me towards him.

I felt like I was a young teen again. Who would have thought it?

"Stop," I said as I pulled away. I put my head against his broad chest, my hand patting his arm. "I can't," I nodded as I stepped back. "I want to, but I can't," I said again, more to myself than him.

"Understood," Gregg nodded.

"Thank you," I nodded as I walked towards the hotel door. "Thank you so much!"

CHRISTMAS MORNING CAME, and we all met in our hotel living room to open presents. I smiled at Gregg, who smiled and nodded back. I told Tony I had met a few old friends from high school. Gregg had said he went on a date with some hot snow bunny.

The laughter filled the room as people opened gifts and sang Christmas songs. The hotel room service brought up our pre-ordered Christmas breakfast. We sat, sang, and laughed for most of the day before hitting the slopes again.

At the dinner downstairs, we shared our table with a couple from out of state, it was joyful, and I forgot about Tony and our impending divorce. I told him last night I wouldn't be forced into a corner, and he told me he wanted no part of me if I couldn't accept all of him.

Gregg passed me in the hallway and stopped me. "Look up," he said.

"Well," I said, looking at the mistletoe. "I can't break the rule, can I?"

"Nope," Gregg said.

We kissed deeply and long. I wanted time to stop right then and there, but it didn't. We quickly stopped as we heard Katy coming around the corner.

"Bye, Mom," she cried as she hugged me.

"Drive safe," I said as I said goodbye to them, including a long hug that lasted too long when I hugged Gregg. I told him Thank you again as he got in the car.

It left Tony and me alone again. I looked at him and smiled. "Who should file?"

"I can do it," Tony said.

"Good," I replied.

I felt my lips as I walked back inside. A long smile crept over my face as I looked at my phone.

'See you next year?' a text read from Gregg.

'Much sooner than that,' I replied. *'A lot sooner!'*

Chapter Two: Good out of Bad

"**W**ell, that was fast," I said as I discovered Jeff had already remarried.

We hadn't been divorced for four months yet, and Jeff was already on his second wife. Teresa, one of my former friends. A self-proclaimed sex addict. I say former because she tried to get with Jeff on multiple occasions.

"She can have him," I shook my head as I unfollowed them on my socials.

I had tried to talk to Jeff before we finalized the divorce, asking if there was middle ground, allowing me to think about his interests, but his mind was made up. So, I gave him the divorce he wanted.

Now he was with her, and I was sure Teresa would give him exactly what he wanted; she was well known within our small circle for trying to steal our husbands and sleeping with any man that would give her attention.

Her infidelity and promiscuity caused rifts in her relationships as her boyfriends would dump her as soon as they found out she cheated; now, she found someone in Jeff who would love it for her to bring someone home.

Teresa had claimed the title of *'hot wife,'* whatever that meant.

"She is just doing it to get you back," Lauren said as we met for lunch.

"I know," I shrugged.

I once told Teresa I would be glad to talk to her about sex addiction after her last boyfriend threw her out of his house. She claimed it was his fault that she slept with his cousin, but that was always her reasoning.

I didn't shrink my friends, as some would call it. My specialty or field of study was bullying, especially in teens and young adults.

I had been bullied as a teenager, which led me to multiple trips to the therapist's office and other dark places.

Having four brothers that teased and mocked me all the time was hard enough; entering puberty earlier than most was even more challenging.

By the time I hit high school, I had a bigger chest than most of the female faculty members, so the names and insults came every day.

"I can't believe he left you the house," Lauren exclaimed.

"He did it so I wouldn't fight him on the boat," I shrugged.

I liked the boat; it was something we both liked to do on a hot summer's day. The lake wasn't too far from our house. We would take it out and have a good time.

"So, he got the boat and the rentals," Lauren shook her head. "It seems you lost that one."

I made more than Jeff, which was alarming for him being a fire investigator for the city. But the schools and the state were cutting down on suicides as our state had skyrocketed to near the top in the nation.

I knew some people made fun of people that got bullied, but it wasn't something to be laughed at or made fun of; for some, it was severe.

"I have the kids," I smiled. "They know their father, and they sided with me."

Jeff hadn't always been the it's my way or the highway type, not when we got together, but after we started our family, that side of him came out quickly. He kept saying that his parents were strict when he was a kid.

'Kids are to be seen and not heard' was his favorite thing to say if the kids got too loud or didn't do as he said.

Frederick, being the oldest, took the brunt of it. When the other two would get in trouble, he would always stand up for them; that's why when he decided to go into the military, I wasn't surprised. Frederick always stood up for anyone that needed it.

"What about the other guy?" Lauren asked.

"What guy?" I asked, knowing who Lauren was talking about, but I wanted her to say it.

"You know the black guy," Lauren said in a whisper.

"You don't have to whisper," I shook my head.

We were in a large restaurant, and no one was near our booth.

"I know, but you know how people are," Lauren shook her head. "Can't say anything without someone getting hurt."

I nodded; it was part of the new world we lived in. While I was an advocate for not bullying, there was definitely a line between saying what you wanted and bullying. If someone said to stop, you stopped. It didn't mean I expected them never to say it, just not to them.

That's where people got the lines crossed. Someone saying you hurt their feelings didn't mean they were soft or wanted you to stop saying how you felt; it just meant that word hurt them. There was a massive difference between the two, but no one wanted to meet in the middle.

Like Jeff, people these days were all about them. The us versus them mentality had taken over everything from politics to religion, raising kids, and even teaching.

If you didn't see it their way, you were the enemy, period! No, if's or but's about it. They were like little children. They started it, so we will end it.

I remember my father saying before he passed away, there was a time when people kept their opinions to themselves, and if you didn't agree with someone, you agreed to disagree and moved the fuck on.

Not today, if you disagreed with someone from the right, you were a lefty and a libtard; if you agreed with someone from the left, you were a bigot or a racist; no middle ground on either.

Lauren, like me, was independent. We viewed things in the gray area. I could see both sides and agreed with many things, but I was told many times. ***"You have to pick a side!"*** My reply was always. ***"No, the fuck I don't!"***

"Well?" Lauren asked.

"Nothing came out of it," I shrugged.

Gregg was way too young for me. We talked a lot after the divorce, mainly online, and that's where I saw a vast difference in opinions and interests.

Gregg liked rap music, which was okay with me, but he liked the new stuff, which I had to say was like nails on a chalkboard to me. I liked the older stuff.

I liked boating and fishing as well as camping. Gregg hated the outdoors. Soon our talks got less and less. And eventually, it just stopped.

"Too bad," Lauren said with her usual smile.

"Why?" I asked.

"You know, would like to have known," Lauren shrugged.

I shook my head. "It's a rumor, trust me," I said.

"How do you know?" Lauren said as she stared at me.

"I just know," I nodded.

"You saw it!" Lauren exclaimed.

I motioned to lower her voice as I looked around.

"Tell me!" Lauren said.

"It was average," I shrugged.

"Just average?" Lauren asked, disappointed.

"Yes, average," I nodded.

"Well, that sucks," Lauren said.

I had seen my fair share of dicks while I was in college, and while I mostly went with girls, some guys piqued my interest, and it was because of that that I knew Gregg was just average, not above, not under, but just average.

We shared some pictures, mostly because he wanted to see my boobs, which I wasn't shy to show him, but that was where our sexual escapades ended.

I had never been shy to show off my chest. I was proud of them. I had never thought about getting a reduction even with the back aches and the stares or the other hundreds of reasons why having huge breasts was a pain.

Mainly because of Jeff. When we first got together, he would plow his dick through them daily. It was a wonder that I even got pregnant as much as he tit fucked me. After Frederick was born, the sex got less, then Dawson came along, and it got less. After Katy was born, we hardly touched each other.

I had fun on the date with Gregg, but I wasn't about to fly for three hours to have sex with someone the same age as my son. It was a fun thought at first, but I wasn't looking for anything, not just yet.

MY DAYS WERE FILLED with appointments and the usual banter with friends. Sometimes I would stay home and video chat with my clients, but some days, I had to go into the office or go to someone's home.

Even meeting some of the people who did the bullying was the usual high and mighty routine. Until they were face to face with me, then it was they didn't mean it to come across that way.

'*Hey mom,*' Dawson texted me as I entered my house after a long day.

'*Hey,*' I replied.

'*Just saw that Jeff moved on. How are you holding up?*' Dawson asked.

Dawson never called his dad, dad; it was always him, that guy, and later on, it became Jeff, which landed him in a lot of trouble with Jeff.

'*I saw it a few days ago,*' I replied. '*I am good, you know your father.*'

'Craig said she's ugly,' Dawson said.

I laughed as I thought about Craig; he would be the one to say it to Jeff's face.

'Everyone has a taste,' I replied.

'That's right, you have to be the shrink,' the reply came, and I knew it was Craig speaking now.

'No, that's the truth,' I replied. *'Everyone has a taste, just because you might think she's ugly, doesn't mean someone else might want to fuck her till her brains turn to mush.'*

'Okay, I can see that,' Craig replied. *'Well, we are here if you need us.'*

I loved my boys, including Mike, even though he acted more like a daughter at times.

Jeff went from a big and tall woman in me to a short and skinny woman in Teresa, but that was Jeff; he wanted someone to bow to his interests.

I gave it a few months tops before he realized that Teresa was only with him so she could sleep with other guys and not be kicked out or dumped. That was why she was with Jeff. Now, she could fuck anyone, and Jeff would like it.

I got myself a puppy, and my neighbor Hank came over and walked it while I was at work, but since I was usually home, it was always under my chair.

I had to remember not to back out too fast, or I rolled over it.

I named him Chuck after my father. Chuck was a rescue that I saw online. Someone found him on the side of the road; his main problem was that he liked to chew on things, including carpets and the sides of the couches.

Since I had an old couch and furniture around the house, I decided to make the guest room Chuck's room, so all the old stuff went in there. That way, he could chew on everything.

"Hey," I said as he bounded toward me when I got home.

The shelter said he would be a huge dog when he grew up, which was fine with me. Growing up, we had large dogs, Rottweilers mainly. My Chuck was a malamute and loved to be hugged.

We settled down to watch some shows, just Chuck and me.

'Some of the girls and I are going to see a show, do you want to come?' Lauren texted me.

Their definition of a show was to go to a male strip club. I had my fill of muscles and baby oil or whatever they used to make their muscles and body glisten under the lights.

Besides, Chuck had found an excellent nestling spot between my legs as I was sprawled out on the couch; the little tyke was fast asleep, and I didn't want to wake him.

'Held captive at the moment, rain check,' I responded with a picture of Chuck.

'Aww, don't blame you, look at the little ears!' Lauren responded.

I knew those ears wouldn't be little for very long; soon, Chuck would take up this whole couch, and I would be the one trying to find space to sit.

After a few hours, I decided to call it a night and head to bed. I put Chuck down in his bed by mine, and we were soon fast asleep.

"SO, THE REASON I BROUGHT you here is I have good news and bad news," my boss Isabella said as we sat at my favorite Italian place for lunch.

I took a deep sigh. "Good news," I said, as I hated getting bad news.

Usually, one of my clients had taken their life after being unable to take the abuse or the bullying. Or that I had to take on more clients.

"I got the promotion," Isabella smiled.

"Nice," I said as we clinked glasses.

Then it dawned on me. "No!" I said, shaking my head.

"Yup, that's the bad news," Isabella smiled. "You got my spot."

I hated dealing with city officials that didn't know a damn thing about mental illness. They only cared about numbers and how many people they could throw at us and *'cure'* them.

Mental illness wasn't something you just came in with and sat down for a few talks and took a few pills and walked out fine.

There were specialists around the world that had been studying this illness for years and still had no clue of the causes, the treatments, or how to prevent someone from thinking ending their life would make all of it go away, yet the moment someone came into the hospital or was carted away, the city and the hospitals looked at us to cure them.

"That means I have to deal with Tyson?" I asked, mentioning the high chief or all the idiots. His term for helping people was to *fix them so they don't go shooting up a school,'* his exact words.

"Yup," Isabella smiled.

"At least I don't have to deal with the governor and his cronies," I shrugged.

"Wait," Isabella said.

I nodded as it finally hit her.

"Fuck!" she said as she sat back in her chair.

"Congrats!" my co-workers screamed as I returned to the clinic.

"Doesn't come into effect until next week," I said as I headed for my new office.

Isabella was already heading home to pack; she would transfer to the new clinic downtown.

I had work to do, most of it was putting some of my clients and patients onto others. We were the number one mental health facility in three states, and in each one, we were understaffed, and patience was wearing thin on most of our therapists, including myself.

I was typing away at my keyboard when the idiot walked into my office.

"Such thing as knocking," I said as I peeped over one of the monitors.

The lovely thing about Isabelle's office was it had two monitors. It took some getting used to, but after a few moments, I had it down.

"We helped finance this building and everything in it," Tyson said as he sat down. "Plus pay all your paychecks."

"So, you don't have any manners," I nodded. "Got it."

We were doing good as a company before the government came along and city officials, but I have to say the massive bump in pay was excellent.

"Let's get one thing straight," Tyson said as he stared at me. "It wasn't my idea. I wanted Kyle."

"That fucking idiot?" I smiled. "Why?"

"He does what he is told, when he is told," Tyson said.

"Plus, he has a dick," I nodded.

"And that's why I didn't want you," Tyson shook his head. "You can't fall in line, follow the chain of command, and you don't listen."

"I do fall in line and the chain of command is for the military, not a mental facility, and we can't *fix* people, we treat the symptoms and help alleviate further outcomes. You want to run all of our clinics like a pharmacy. Come in get meds, take meds and be perfectly fine, that's not how this works."

"Trust me," Tyson said. "If I had my way, that's exactly how it would work."

I wanted to throw both monitors at his perfectly shaped head.

"Tell me, how would that work, exactly," I said, folding my arms and staring at him.

"All this talk about mental illness is bullshit!" Tyson said. "It's an excuse for people that can't handle the real world. I would force them into it, and if they didn't, I would lock them up with all the others."

I laughed. "Glad it's not up to you, because half of this country would be in prison," I said. "All of us have some mental bullshit we put up with every day, even you. The difference between them and us is our brains are wired differently, they can't help who they are, and what they feel."

"Says the person getting paid to say exactly that," Tyson responded.

We had a staring match for a few moments before he got up.

"I bet you think it's okay that a child molester thinks they have an illness too," he said as he headed for the door.

"No, I don't, I think it's more than that," I shook my head, "but I do believe that napoleon passed his short man syndrome to most of the short men around the world."

Instantly Tyson stopped at the door. "Keep going," I nodded.

Tyson hated it when people made fun of his height.

"YOU DID NOT!" ISABELLA said as we talked on the phone later that day.

"Yup," I replied.

"Cynthia! He is your boss!" Isabelle shouted.

"Don't care," I nodded as I was making dinner. "He went low with that child molester comment, so I went lower," I smiled.

I had no problem going to the gutter with people who thought they were better than me or anyone else. We were all equal, and all of us were trying to get to the next day and the day after.

"He is going to get you back," Isabella said.

"Jeff thought the same thing," I shrugged. "I was in a family of mostly men, I can take care of myself."

"He really hates it when people make fun of his height," Isabella said.

"That's okay," I said, trying not to step on my shadow. "Chuck kiddo, you can't step between mummy's legs."

"Chuck?" Isabella asked.

"Yeah, I got a puppy," I sighed as I stared down at the small pup with its gray eyes staring up at me. "We are still in the getting to know each other phase," I smiled as I picked Chuck up and placed him on the table. "There."

"You're full of surprises," Isabella said.

I stared behind me at Chuck, staring down at the floor.

"Yeah, I know," I smiled as I knew the poor guy was estimating if he could jump down from the table as he paced back and forth.

"Well, I better go," Isabella said.

I hung up and stared at Chuck. "It's a long way down, for a small pup, I wouldn't risk it if I were you."

I knew putting him up there would come and bite me in the ass further down the road, but at least I could move around the kitchen freely now.

Another night, and another night alone with my dog. I was starting to get used to it.

Chapter Three: New and Old Friends

"You know they don't talk, right?" I smiled at the teenager behind the counter at the movie theatre desk.

"Sorry," the young smiled as he gave me my ticket stub.

"You didn't have to embarrass the guy," Katy said as we walked into the movie theatre.

"He was embarrassing himself by staring," I replied.

Katy didn't know what it was like to be heavy-chested; the moment her chest got big, she went straight to the doctor and got them reduced; she was eighteen.

If she had been me, they would have been double their size. Poor Katy had D's and decided they were too big for her petite frame. I was that size before entering high school.

"That's why I am glad Mike doesn't like big ones," Katy shrugged.

Mike didn't like big ones because he was a small man with small hands. When I met Jeff, he used to say anything bigger than a handful was a waste; after he met me, that quickly changed.

I had flown out to see Katy as she announced she was pregnant and that I would soon be a grandma. Knowing that Frederick hadn't had a girlfriend since high school and Dawson was gay, this was my only opportunity to be a grandma.

I knew friends that were grandmas to five or six kids at forty. I was turning forty-four next month, and Katy's soon-to-be child would be my first grandkid. I had already planned to spoil it rotten.

"Do you ever think about...." Katy started to say.

"Nope," I shook my head.

"Never?" Katy asked.

"Not once," I replied.

Not through back pain or anything had I ever had the inclination to go through a reduction. My mom had big boobs, and so did my aunts and my grandma; every woman on my mother's side had huge boobs, and if Katy hadn't sliced and diced hers, she would probably be bigger also.

"I couldn't imagine being any bigger," Katy said.

Sometimes I admired the smaller chests of women. An example was Katy. I could never wear something like she was wearing, something strapless and braless. I would fall out and cause a scene.

I guess that's why most women in movies like the one we were watching were small-chested so that they could have scenes like this one. Walking through a house with only a bra and panties while dancing. No movie would show a woman like me doing that; there would be an uproar.

Even most people hated that women like me were proud of our figures. I was a big woman, both tall and wide, with huge hips, thighs, ass, and boobs.

Katy got a lot of stares from guys as she was stunning, slim, or petite, as some would say, with small but perky breasts and a nice pert ass.

Too bad for them, Katy was very loyal to Mike; she had no male friends and talked about him constantly.

I was glad they had waited until they were both in their second year of college to get pregnant. They had plans for both to stay in college and finish their classes.

I was going to help as much as possible to ensure they kept to their plans.

Mike wanted to be an exotic animal veterinarian specializing in reptiles. He had a fixation on crocodiles and alligators but also wanted to do snakes and others.

Katy wanted to specialize in engineering, which wasn't a surprise for me as she always wanted to take apart things as a child and put them back together.

WHILE SEEING MY DAUGHTER and spending time with her was nice, I was glad to return home.

Hank had taken Chuck for the weekend, and the moment I got home, all I wanted to do was spend time with my dog.

"You love him more than you love us," Katy said as we talked online via video call.

I wouldn't say that out loud, but I loved watching Chuck do his thing. The puppy made me laugh like no one else ever did; as I talked to my daughter, I looked down at him, staring at a spider crawling up the wall. His ears perked up, and his head tilted to the side as he watched the tiny insect.

"If it's a girl we are going to call her Laci," Katy said as I saw Mike walking back and forth in the background.

I spent some money and got them a nice starter family house close to the college. I was pleased that they had level heads. Mike was taking night classes while Katy was doing morning classes; this way, both would be there for the baby.

"After my mother, that's nice," I nodded. "And if it's a boy?"

"Douglas, after Mike's father," Katy nodded.

"That's fair," I smiled.

"I better get going," Katy said.

"Yeah, I better get ready," I nodded.

I had turned down my friend's invitations for too long. Tonight I promised I would go out to the club with them.

"AND YOU SAY YOU AREN'T on the prowl," Judy said as she saw me exit my vehicle.

"What?" I replied.

I had met Lauren to pick her up so she could be the designated driver to return home. If I was going out on the town. I was going to drink.

"Look at you!" Judy said as we walked to the woman's club.

I decided to wear my nice club clothes. I didn't think I would fit in these black jeans that hugged my legs, thighs, and ass like a second skin and a black mesh top, it had an undergarment built in, but it showed a lot more cleavage than I would usually show on any given day.

The mesh was completely see-through and showed the girls with every step, my chest bounced and swayed.

"Joy is going to have a heart attack," Judy said as we showed our ID's at the door.

"Good," I replied.

Joy was the one member of our group that I didn't get along with; we butted heads on many things.

"Wow," I said as I entered the nightclub.

"Right," Lauren smiled.

Now I knew why they spent so much time here. The guys dancing were hunks. Muscular, tanned, and completely naked hunks.

"Cynthia, this way," Judy said as she pulled me towards their table.

I couldn't stop staring at the tall, muscular figure of one of the men. He had muscles and a very nice cock.

"Oh," Joy said as we got to the table, and she saw what I was wearing.

"Yeah, oh," I said as I sat down.

"You two behave," Michelle said, "We are here to have a good time and that's what we are going to do."

"Yes Mom," I smiled.

The five of us talked a lot but mostly stared at the men dancing around us. Especially the oiled-up fellas that brought out our drinks.

Michelle was always the one that brought out the life of the party.

"Excuse me?" Michelle asked one of the hunks. "Is Vince working tonight?"

"Yes, he should be on next," he said as he returned to dancing.

"Who is Vince?" I asked.

"Oh, you will see," Lauren smiled. "And remember what you said about that being a rumor," she said with a wink.

The music changed, and this tall black man dressed in a tuxedo with a top hat emerged. I almost laughed as he danced sexy to a classical song.

Then as clothes came off and I saw what lay underneath it.

"Holy," I said, staring at what could only be described as a third leg.

"Just a rumor huh?" Lauren said as we were all standing and clapping.

"Motherfucker," I said with wide eyes open as he approached our table.

I had thought it was some appendage or something he had strapped onto himself, but it was swinging and pulsing as he approached us.

"That's his fucking cock," I said as I watched it.

"Yup," Judy said as she jumped up and down and started putting dollar bills into his strap.

Judy was the benchmark for stay-at-home mom of the year. She had three kids, two dogs, and a cat. Her husband Benson was a structural engineer and was as nerdy as possible, and she loved him, but if Benson could see his library wife now, he wouldn't recognize her.

"Big fucking cock!" Judy said as she peered over her glasses and shouted at him.

Michelle and Joy were right there beside her.

"Say something," Lauren said as I was still awestruck.

"It's a huge fucking cock!" I said as if my mind was stuck on repeat.

It wasn't just long, it was thick, and the head was thick and purple looking; it looked angry.

All I could think about was how big it was. How would it feel in my mouth? Could I get it down my throat? What if I got on top? How far could I sit on it before I called it quits? Did it hurt him with all that blood rushing to that thing?

"Cynthia!" Joy said, slapping my hand. "We can't touch!"

"But..." I said as I saw my hand reaching out to grab it. "I want to," I said.

Then he was gone to the other side of the long winding stage.

I shook my head and was brought back to reality.

"Damn!" I said as I realized I had made a fool of myself.

"Don't worry it happens all the time," a voice said from behind.

I was shocked to see who was standing in front of me.

"Cat got your tongue?" the redhead asked.

"Roxxy?" I said.

"That's me," Roxxy said.

I hadn't seen this woman since my third year in college.

"What are you doing here?" I asked as we finished hugging, and we sat down.

"Roxxy owns this place," Lauren smiled.

"Yeah, right," I smiled.

"No, blondie, I do," Roxxy nodded at me.

"No way!" I said, looking around at the other private stages and the long and well-lit bar.

"Yeah, lock, stock and barrel," Roxxy nodded.

Roxxy was the one that got me to play for the other side. It was a dare, and I had to say a good one. Roxxy found pleasure centers in and on my body that no man past, present, or future would ever find.

"Last time I saw you, you were trying to save the whales," I said, shaking my head.

"It's a long story, blondie," Roxxy said as she stood up. "But I got to make my rounds, stick around and I might tell you it."

"Blondie?" Joy asked.

I smiled as Roxxy left.

"I dyed my hair in college," I shrugged. "Was tired of being called a ginger, so for most of my college years I was blonde."

The rest of the night went well; even though I saw a few other hunks, my mind was set on hearing Roxy's story. I never told many people about my college years, but if I did, Roxxy would be the main part of that story; she and I were inseparable until I met Tony.

JOY VOLUNTEERED TO take Lauren home, and I stuck around until closing.

"Really want to hear that story, huh?" Roxxy asked as she led me to her office.

"Definitely," I said as I followed behind her, just like in college. I always followed her like a good lap dog.

Roxxy was always the ringleader of our group; even the guys would fall in line behind her. Roxxy bowed down to no one.

"Take a seat," Roxxy said.

Roxxy and I were together for years, even though I slept with many women; it was because Roxxy told me to; when she said jump, I just jumped.

"I see a lot has changed," I said, looking over at Roxxy.

She had always been a redhead, but she was as skinny as a bean pole and flat-chested back then. Now she had massive boobs and a rocking body.

"Most of it is store bought," Roxxy said, sitting down.

Roxxy told me about what happened when I took off and left college when I met Tony.

I was just like Katy; I fell hard when I fell for Tony. The women in my family always fell in love hard; my mom left her small town for my trucker father and her mother before, and so on.

It was part of our nature to fall in love and do anything for the person we loved; that's why Roxxy was still a huge influence in my life.

Roxxy told me about her adventures, from being on an anti-waler ship to visiting the rainforests to try and save them to saving the baby seals; she had lived a full life.

"Then, when my father was on his death bed, he told me to revisit the places I had been and see the world from the other side," Roxxy said. "So, I did."

"What happened?" I asked.

"None of it mattered," Roxxy shook her head. "None of the rioting, protesting, hashtags, flags, none of it, mattered."

I looked over at her.

"People put their signs up in their yards, or stickers on their cars," Roxxy said, shaking her head. "Vote for this person, lock this person up, hashtag this, hashtag that, pro choice, pro life, at the end of the fucking day, none of it matters," Roxxy shrugged. "Your pitiful opinion means jack shit! So, I decided I would no longer be a lemming."

I smiled at that.

"I said Fuck them, fuck all of them, right, left, in-between, all of it. Fuck it all!" Roxxy smiled. "They think putting a flag on their big truck matters, no the fuck it doesn't, it will not change a goddamn thing! Think taking guns away will change, nope, if someone wants to kill another person, there isn't a damn thing you can do about it, until after it's done. Sure, you can say well because another person had their gun, we stopped them from killing anyone else. Yeah, you did, but that first person is still dead as a doornail, huh? And most likely that was the original target, so in the end you didn't stop shit!"

I liked when Roxxy got like this; she was still the woman I fell for the first year of college.

"So, much crap in the world and people are worrying about what is SJW, Racist, Bigots, or Snowflakes. Who the fuck cares?" Roxxy said. "There is so much other bullshit you could worry about, but you care about who is sleeping with who, and how someone feels, or what they identify as, Fuck you!" Roxxy said.

"I dare any of them to jump in their car and drive around the country, with just the cash in their pocket or wallet. Don't take any more money out, no planning, no destination itinerary or anything just go, but you have to visit every state at least once, and not drive through it, go around each state. Then they will see there is a much bigger problem than just left or right," Roxxy sat back in her chair.

"So, that's when you stopped?" I asked.

"I didn't just stop, babe, I quit," Roxxy said. "I quit everything. Haven't voted in years. I couldn't care less who is sitting in office or what they are doing, could care less about anything but these four walls, and my life has been perfect because of it," Roxxy smiled.

I sat back and smiled.

"What about you?" Roxxy leaned forward. "Really think you are making a difference helping people with their troubles?"

"I, well there are good days and bad, just like anything else," I shrugged.

"Bullshit," Roxxy said. "Mental illness is one of those things that will never go away, but if you want to try and treat it, go for it."

"So, we should what, let them be?" I asked.

"Never said that, I said it will never go away, treating the symptoms is like putting your finger in a cracked damn, eventually it's going to break," Roxxy shrugged.

"So, pull my finger out and let it break?" I asked.

"Yup," Roxxy nodded. "Easier to clean up the mess afterward."

"You haven't changed," I smiled.

"You know where most of those people end up right?" Roxxy asked.

"Here," I nodded.

"Yup, I've heard it all from men and women," Roxxy smiled. "Easier to treat what bothers you with alcohol and naked men and women dancing."

"I didn't see any women," I said.

"Across the street," Roxxy smiled. "I own that club too."

"Get the fuck out," I smiled.

"Sex sells," Roxxy shrugged. "You know else comes in these places?"

I shook my head.

"Politicians," Roxxy winked at me. "Sure, they try to hide themselves, but a few well known, and supposedly straight politicians have walked through that door and spent a lot of money watching other men strip in front of them."

"And you have bent a few ears," I nodded.

"Just because I don't vote doesn't mean I haven't bent a few things in my favor," Roxxy smiled. "Like I said, sex sells. I own a few websites, dating apps, and some let's say adult themed movie studios."

"Roxxy!" I smiled.

"Only two things really matter in this world, sex and religion, in that order," Roxxy smiled. "I decided I would get a foothold in one, and you know I couldn't be religious to save my life."

I sat back in my chair.

"So, what do you say?" Roxxy asked.

"What do you mean?" I replied.

"Join me," Roxxy said. "I need a manager for my club across the street."

"I couldn't," I shook my head.

"You could," Roxxy said. "You would do more for your clinics sitting on this side of this desk than behind yours."

I sat still for a moment.

"Tell you what," Roxxy said, standing up. "I will give you to the end of the week to think about it."

"Okay," I nodded.

"It was nice seeing you again, blondie," Roxxy said as we shook hands.

"You too," I smiled.

I left and returned home with a lot to think about and good memories.

'Just something to help with your decision,' Roxxy texted me. There was an image that I couldn't look at while driving.

"Holy fuck!" I said as I looked it up as I pulled into my driveway.

It was a picture of Vince's cock.

Chapter Four: A Step Forward

"Not dealing with you today," I shook my head as I walked into my office Monday morning.

Tyson was already at my office door waiting for me.

"You know the workday starts at eight," Tyson said.

"Yes, I know," I replied.

"It's eight-ten," Tyson said, staring at his watch.

"I ran into traffic," I said, opening my door.

"Then leave home earlier," Tyson said, barging into my office.

"Make yourself at home," I smiled as I put my stuff on the large couch.

"Did you hear the news?" Tyson said as he threw a newspaper onto my desk.

"Yes," I said, looking at the headlines.

Another teen ended their life yesterday by walking in front of a city bus.

"Not the best way to go," I said.

"Not funny," Tyson said, "Keep reading."

I turned the paper toward me and smiled.

"Told you," I said, pushing the paper back toward him. "You can't treat these people like they have a cold, or the flu."

"One of our clinics released him four days ago," Tyson said. "Both sides of the media are having a field day, it's the first time both sides have agreed on anything."

"Because they are both right," I shrugged. "You and your bosses think we can completely cure depression, suicide, or any number of mental illnesses with a few sit down sessions and some pills. It doesn't work that way."

"So, we are supposed to keep them institutionalized forever?" Tyson asked as he stared at the paper. "Who is going to pay for that?"

"How many people saw him get splattered across the sidewalk?" I asked. "You tell me how they get that image out of their head and I will tell you how long we should keep them around for."

Tyson sighed. "His father is a well-known member of the community."

"You mean he is rich," I said.

"And has powerful friends," Tyson said. "They want answers."

"Then give it to them," I shrugged. "You're the one that wants us to release them after two weeks, whether we agree or not."

"Did he spend the full two weeks?" Tyson asked.

"One week, six days," I said as I looked him up on my screen. "Oh, your favorite therapist Kyle Knoxx was the one to sign the discharge papers. With notes to seek additional help and care."

"Dammit," Tyson said as he stood up.

"Should have listened, we need more time," I said. "He was dealing with his mum's death, by you guessed it, suicide," I shook my head. "Like mother like son, she jumped in front of a train."

"They are going to have my head," Tyson said as he paced back and forth.

"Good luck with that," I smiled. "Now kindly leave my office."

My day was filled with emails and calls about the young teen and how we could have prevented it. But there was nothing that we could have done with our hands tied.

I talked to the father, and he was irate but surprisingly calm at the same time. It was like a weight had been lifted off him. Sure, he missed his wife and son, but the calm, knowing that they were gone and he didn't need to worry anymore, made him calm.

I had seen it before in many family members after a family member died of cancer or any other mental disease. After the initial grief period, there was a strange calm in knowing they didn't have to worry about them anymore, that they weren't suffering or had to take medications.

"You have a visitor," Alice said as she peeked into my office.

I motioned to let them in, and Roxxy walked through the door.

I smiled as I saw her wearing a short black skirt with black leather thigh-high boots and a crop top that barely held her enormous tits in check.

I couldn't believe she had gone that big from flat-chested in college to grapefruit-sized tits on her chest. I was sure they cost a fortune.

"I am sure you made an impression on everybody in the lobby." I shook my head as she sat down.

"I think that's why your receptionist put me to the front of the line," Roxxy smiled.

"Yeah, I can see why," I said, looking at her.

"So, this is where you save the world?" Roxxy asked as she looked around my office.

"Yeah," I said, slightly happy with myself. "It's not the bat cave but it works for me."

"Not the type of office you will have, but it's nice," Roxxy said.

"I saw your office, this is much better," I replied.

"But does it have naked men or women outside," Roxxy responded.

"No," I smiled back at her.

"I rest my case," Roxxy shrugged.

"So, what brings you down here?" I asked.

"I was going to see Vince perform, thought I would come and see you, see how the other side worked," Roxxy replied.

"Vince, does what exactly?" I asked. Thinking of the man behind the massive cock.

"Well, it's not any show on Broadway," Roxxy laughed. "He is at the porn studio."

"Wait," I said, nearly coughing on my coffee. "He does porn?"

"What did you think he did, surely you don't think stripping is his only job?" Roxxy said.

"No, of course not, but I didn't think it would be porn," I said, trying to think about the poor woman that tried to take that massive cock inside of any orifice.

I had a moment of weakness looking at the damn thing, but I never thought about sucking on it or even trying to have it inside me.

"He is doing an anal scene today," Roxxy said with a huge smile. "Do you want to go see?"

"No," I shook my head quickly. "No, there is no way, in the... really?" I asked, thinking about someone taking that black cock in their ass.

"You know you want to," Roxxy said as she stood up.

"Okay, fine," I said, standing up and joining her.

"HOLY FUCK," I SAID as I saw the pale-skinned skinny girl flat on her back as Vince shoved his cock into her mouth.

"Told ya," Roxxy smiled.

"No fucking way," I tilted my head to the side and watched her throat bulge upward as Vince's cock disappeared into her mouth.

"Yup, all of it," Roxxy said proudly. "Daddy issues."

"What?" I asked.

"She has daddy issues," Roxxy nodded. "We found her online doing her amateur thing, while living in the same house as her father."

"Uh huh," I said as Vince started ramming his cock in and out of her mouth. "She must have no gag reflex at all!" I said, holding my throat as I saw hers bulge upward again.

"You're not listening," Roxxy said as she nudged me.

"What?" I replied.

"Daddy issues," Roxxy nodded at the blonde on the bed.

"I am sure of it," I replied. "Most of them do. Or ex -husbands or brothers, or just nymphos."

"Sex addicts," Roxxy corrected me. "They don't like being called nymphs anymore."

"Right," I nodded back. "Whatever the case maybe, that's why a lot of women get into porn."

"Sex workers," Roxxy corrected again. "They don't like porn stars or porn or adult entertainer. Sex workers is the correct term these days."

"Oh, whatever, it's getting paid to have sex," I replied. "Or implied sex, or stripping. Do we really have to have a name for all of it?"

"They do," Roxxy shrugged.

"So, what's your point?" I asked as the two got into position.

"Nothing, just saying, you could still do your job, while doing this," Roxxy said.

Again, I tilted my head the other way and moved slightly forward out of my chair. I watched as the head of his massive cock pierced her hole.

"She will never shit properly again," I said as I watched the cock enter her ass.

"Cynthia!" Roxxy exclaimed.

"I am just saying," I shrugged.

There was no way that massive cock wasn't doing some internal damage. He held her arms back and used them to pull her skinny body back and forth on his thick, long cock as it pummeled her ass.

I had done anal a few times, and for a while, I couldn't sit properly or go to the bathroom was a pain as it hurt a lot more than it should, but then it went away, so maybe if she didn't do it again for a while things might be okay.

"Fuck no!" I shook my head as I saw the large gaping hole of her ass. As he took his cock out, and she held her asshole open for him to put it back in. "I'm out!"

A few people laughed as I walked out of the studio and into the other room.

"You, okay?" Roxxy caught up to me outside in the parking lot.

"First, no way in hell am I going to look at his cock the same ever again," I said, shaking my head. That was not a cock. It was a battering ram.

"Second why would anyone do that to their body?"

I could see way down into her asshole that was not a turn-on at all.

Roxxy smiled. "Let's get something to eat."

"I SAY DO IT," LAUREN said as she came to my house for drinks later that night.

"Did you not hear the part with the large gaping hole?" I said as I drank.

"It's called gaping," Lauren nodded. "It's a fetish, there are lots of them online, each one trying to take larger things into their asses."

"Get the fuck out!" I shouted.

"Nope, one of my ex's had tons of videos of women riding these massive dildos and shoving huge things up their asses."

"I think my ass just tightened even more," I replied.

Lauren laughed. "But seriously, take the job," she smiled at me. "You're miserable where you are, and everyone knows it."

"So, everyone is talking about me and about my misery?" I asked.

"Not about your misery, but yes," Lauren nodded.

"I don't know how to take that," I replied, standing up and looking at the backyard.

We were on the deck at the back of my house. I loved that my backyard backed against the wooded area of our housing complex.

"Jeff has moved on," Lauren said as she hugged me from behind. "Your kids are happy, all of them. So, when do you get to be happy?"

I put my head against hers and nodded.

"We did make a good couple for a while, though, right?" thinking back to the first day Jeff and I bought this house.

Frederick was two at the time. The deck hadn't been built yet. We thought we would spend the rest of our lives together in this house.

"You two raised good kids and even better adults," Lauren said as she rubbed my arms. "Now, it's time for you to be happy, take the damn job!"

After Lauren left, I thought about it. I had always put my family first; my job paid well and was good enough to help put my kids through college and pay for anything they wanted. They never had to want for anything; we never struggled to pay bills or live paycheck to paycheck. We had it all because Jeff and I worked hard to ensure they got the best.

I enjoyed it and felt good helping people, but I was never happy with it.

Jeff liked being the hero and helping people. Now he enjoyed sitting behind a desk and only going in after the fire was out.

"Fuck it," I said as I turned over in bed.

"YOU WHAT?" TYSON ASKED as I started packing my stuff.

"Quit," I repeated. "You know the thing where people don't want to put up with other people's bullshit anymore."

"You can't quit," Tyson said, shaking his head.

"I definitely can, and I am doing it. Watch me!" I said as I started heading for the door.

"I mean you can't because we have no one to take your place," Tyson said as he stared at me.

"You wanted Kyle, right, hire him," I shrugged.

"Kyle quit after that kid and the bus," Tyson said. "So did Isabella."

"Ha!" I laughed. "Isabella quit also."

"The mayor wanted to find a scapegoat and before he could, she quit," Tyson said reluctantly.

"Smart woman," I nodded. "And also, not my problem, You know why? Because I quit!"

I walked out of the office and strolled out of the building.

"Damn that felt good!" I said as I got in my car.

It felt good to look him straight in the eye and say those words. Even better was walking out of that building. Now all I had to do was see Roxxy.

"To quitting!" Roxxy said as we clinked cocktail glasses.

"Yeah," I said as I looked around the club.

"So, what do you think?" Roxxy asked.

"Do I get to pick?" I asked.

"Absolutely, the guys or the girls?" Roxxy asked.

I looked around, and while I thought I would enjoy scantily clad men with muscles and glistening oily bodies walking around me all day, it was starting to get boring.

"Girls," I nodded.

"Good," Roxxy smiled. "They get whiney and have way too many problems. You might regret quitting the therapy job after a few of them come to you with their attitudes, and feelings."

"Fuck!" I said as I forgot about how whiney some women could get. "Redo?"

"Nope," Roxxy said. "Men are way easier to handle, they keep most of that shit to themselves. I just have to deal with egos."

"Goddamit!" I couldn't believe Roxxy had fooled me.

"Have fun," Roxxy said as I stood up.

I held up my middle finger as I drank the last of my drink, then headed across the road.

Roxxy had already done the introductions, so all I had to do was take over.

While in high school, I worked for a diner, then in college, I managed a shoe store and a campus café, so this was new to me.

"So, you're her," a lady said as she entered my new office.

"Eliza, I presume," I said as I looked at the tall black woman standing before me.

"That would be correct," Eliza said.

Eliza had been managing things after the last manager retired.

"Why didn't you ask to be manager?" I asked, sitting back in my chair.

"Of these bitches?" Eliza smiled. "No fucking way."

I shook my head.

"Yup, Roxxy saw the large sticker that sucker plastered all over your forehead," Eliza smiled. "So, let's talk."

Eliza filled me in on all the things going on in the nightclub, from secret blow jobs to whose baby daddy was fucking other women and everything else.

By the end of the talk, I felt like I had been thrown back into high school.

"Drama," I nodded.

"Shit, ton," Eliza responded. "So, whatever you drink, make sure Toni has it well stocked because you will need all of it."

THE FIRST NIGHT I KEPT the club closed as I wanted to talk to everyone and ensure we were on the same page. Some didn't like the idea that I was putting up new cameras, especially in the area where most had been giving blow jobs to clients.

I wasn't about to be raided, and the cops found some bleach blonde going down on some old guy that could barely get it up.

Then I told them I would be taking some of the money I was paying them to fund a day and night care service. Lauren's daughter had volunteered to offer her daycare services to those that needed it, and since most of them were new mothers or had kids, it went over very well. I told them I would be raising the prices of the drinks as well, so that would go into the funds as well.

I didn't get much pushback, and they also brought up some good points, like the bounces were letting in their friends for free and letting some of them get a little too handsy. That meant a talk with the bouncers the hour after the girls.

I separated them because of what Eliza had said; the bouncers and girls didn't get along. Toni's only argument was the liquor guy was a creep. I smiled at that challenge.

The talk with the bouncers didn't go well at all. Eliza warned me that it wouldn't; they wanted more of the cut from the drinks and didn't want to pay into the fund for the girls, which I told them was debatable if they didn't let their friends in for free.

All in all, it was a long night.

"Told you," Eliza said.

"Hit me again," I said as Eliza poured me another drink.

"Roxxy sure pulled the wool over your eyes," Eliza smiled.

"She sure did," I smiled. "Tell me there has to be a good thing about all this?"

"Oh yeah," Eliza said. "The money."

"Even with the drink hike?" I asked.

"Please, the fools that come in here?" Eliza smiled. "The other strip clubs are shit holes, with watered down drinks, shitty atmosphere, trailer park girls that are way too trashy, plus they are situated in very bad neighborhoods, and I mean the hood part of neighbor. If you catch my drift."

I knew what she was talking about.

"We have the airport three miles from here," Eliza said. "Four upscale hotels just down the road, the football stadium is a ten-minute drive, plus there is a cop station around the corner, and they come in once or twice a night just to say hey," Eliza said. "You will do good to get into their good graces."

"Good," I nodded as I stood up to leave. "Oh, you remember how I got suckered into this?"

"Yes," Eliza smiled.

"Congrats, you just got promoted to assistant," I laughed as I walked away.

"Cynthia take that back," Eliza said. "Cynthia! Don't walk away from me, take that back!"

"See you tomorrow, assistant," I waved back at her.

"You white bitch!" Eliza smiled.

Chapter Five: Finding Happiness.

The first few weeks were a bit rough. Getting the hang of being a manager for a strip club wasn't as easy as I thought it would be.

First, it was managing schedules, then as soon as the ladies found out that I used to be a therapist, they all came to me with their problems.

"How many times Stephanie!" I yelled as I went to the back room and found Stephanie's blonde hair bouncing up and down on one of the bouncer's cock.

I grabbed her head and shoved it down hard. "If you are going to suck a cock," I said, holding her head down. "Suck it properly, or don't do it all!"

Leeroy smiled at me as poor Stephanie's hands flayed about as I held her head.

"Leeroy," I smiled at the tall white bouncer with full-body tattoos. "I need you to work tomorrow night," I said, not caring about Stephanie and arms waving about like she was about to drown.

"Cynthia," Leeroy smiled. "I would love to but...."

I took Stephanie's head off his cock by yanking her blonde hair.

"You stupid bitch! I couldn't...." Stephanie tried to say.

"Sure," Leeroy smiled. "Anything you want."

I shoved Stephanie's head back down. "Continue," I said as I walked away.

If it wasn't one thing, it was another.

"The cops are back," Eliza said as we walked down the corridor.

"Is Melanie working tonight?" I asked, not breaking my stride.

"Of course," Eliza replied.

I nodded as I walked out into the main area. The flashing lights and the girls dancing were always a spectacle. I walked towards the officers.

"We hear that..." one of the officers started saying.

"She will be right out," I said, holding up my hand at them. "And fellas the next time you want to come and see Melanie, don't come in uniform it scares the higher paying clients."

I shook my head as Melanie's entrance music hit.

Melanie was the star attraction. A young country girl with huge natural tits that nearly rivaled my own, the moment she came out dressed in daisy duke shorts and a plaid shirt tied in the knot, the officers sat down.

"To be young again," I smiled as I saw Melanie dancing as her perky tits bounced everywhere.

Roxxy met me in the office.

"So," she smiled at me.

"It's getting better," I said as I looked out the large one-way window.

Melanie was walking across the stage towards the cops.

"I have a present for you," Roxxy said, throwing a yellow folder across the table.

I opened it and smiled. "Oh, this is good," I said, looking at the pictures. "Really good."

"Told you having a place like this has its perks," Roxxy winked.

THE FOLLOWING DAY I stood outside the large glass building that held most of the city's influential people's offices.

"Hi Daniel," I casually said as my victim exited his chauffeured black car and started walking up the steps.

"Cynthia," Daniel casually replied as he stared at his phone.

"Would like to talk to you," I said.

"Don't have time," Daniel said without stopping. "Other important things to do, than talk to...."

He stopped immediately as he tried to walk past me and was about to enter the building. I had hit send on my phone.

"If you want to talk about that image and all the others," I said as I walked back up the steps toward him as many busy people walked up and down the stairs around us. "And there are a lot more images," I smiled. "You know where I will be."

I grinned as I walked down the stairs.

"Cynthia!" Daniel yelled as I disappeared into the large crowd.

Daniel didn't take long to walk into the bagel shop down the block from the office building.

"That was fast," I smiled as Daniel sat before me.

"I never thought you would be the type," Daniel said. "I share that cloud account with Debra," he said, waving the waiter away. "You're lucky she didn't see it."

"You mean you are lucky," I replied.

"How did you get it?" Daniel asked.

"Them," I corrected. "Them, is the correct word."

"Don't play with me!" Daniel responded, slamming his fist onto the table.

"Temper, temper," I smiled. "Now you know how they feel," I shrugged. "The people you and your cronies in that building of yours think the medical field can treat with a simple sit and talk and a brush of the hand. They feel helpless."

"Not this again," Daniel said. "I told Derek and Tyson to deal with this, why are you coming to me?"

"Because you're their boss," I said. "And...."

I turned my phone to show another image.

"Stop it!" Daniel said, lowering my phone. "What do you want?"

"Let the medical field do their jobs," I replied. "That's it, if they say they need more time, they need more time. You don't like feeling like this, I can see it in your hand movements, your eyes are twitching and your...."

"Don't do that," Daniel said in disgust as he sat back in his chair. "Don't diagnose me, like I am one of them," he said, sitting uncomfortably in the chair. "Fine, I will get the ball rolling, anything else?"

"Yes, Tyson he needs to be gone by the end of the day," I smiled.

"Fine," Daniel replied. "Anything else?"

"No," I nodded.

"Good," Daniel replied as he stood up. "I knew you had it in you," he said, straightening his suit and tie.

"What's that?" I asked.

"The ability to play in the big leagues," Daniel smiled. "You ever want a job in the office, you let me know."

"No, thanks," I shook my head. "A friend said it's easier and less messy to play down here."

"Yes, but messy is where the fun is," Daniel smiled as he bent down and kissed my cheek. *"And the big money,"* he whispered in my ear.

"No, thanks," I replied, looking at him.

"I want confirmation those images are deleted," Daniel said as he walked away.

"Soon as I get confirmation of what I want," I smiled back.

"End of the day," Daniel smiled. "Oh, Debra is having some baking thing going on at the church in a week. She wanted to know if you are still coming?"

"Wouldn't miss it," I smiled.

Daniel walked out into the bustle of the city without a care in the world.

I looked at the images on my phone. Only if Debra could see these, her husband hugging and kissing a younger man and grabbing the young man's crotch while at a male strip club.

"Poor Debra," I said as I put my phone away.

"YOU FUCKING BITCH!" Tyson yelled at me over the phone.

"Damn that was fast," I replied.

I had barely made it to my office before Tyson called me.

"So, it was you!" Tyson yelled.

"Yup," I replied.

"You are a traitorous, fat bitch!" Trevor shouted.

"Fat, I will give you, but traitorous, come on, you can do better than that," I smiled as I walked past my workers as I went up to my office.

I held my phone away from my ear as Tyson uttered a string of insults.

"Feel better?" I asked as I sat down.

"I have a family that I provide for," Tyson said.

"Again, so do those people you sweep under the rug," I said. "Well swept, since you don't work for the city no more."

More insults went flying.

"I just wanted to bring you down to their level," I shrugged. "I might not work for them anymore, but I am still going to help them."

"I will find a new job and I swear every single one of those mental idiots, I come across I will bury under so much...." Tyson said.

I hung up. "Idiot," I smiled.

"You look happy," Eliza said as she entered my office.

"Extremely," I smiled.

"You had a visitor," Eliza said as she threw a large envelope on my table. "They just wanted to drop this off."

I opened it. "That was very fast," I smiled as I reviewed the documents.

"Anything I should be worried about?" Eliza asked.

"Nope, I promise," I replied.

"Good," Eliza said. "I don't like being caught up in your white people affairs."

Eliza smiled. I shook my head. "How's Edward? Or baby daddy number two, or is it three?" I asked as Eliza walked away.

"Oh, shut the fuck up!" Eliza said.

I laughed as she gave me the finger.

She hated when I brought up her kid's fathers.

I deleted all the images off my phone, then pulled out the yellow folder with the pictures, took a picture of them burning in my trash can, and sent it to Daniel.

'Glad to do business with you,' Daniel responded.

'You too,' I replied.

Roxxy was right; it was nice getting my way without getting my hands too dirty.

I felt like celebrating; more than that, I felt the need for some male company. Now that I was single, I knew someone I had always wanted to play with, but Tony would have killed me if I had tried.

"WINSTON DOESN'T WORK here anymore," one of the guys at the firehouse said as I came around.

"Since when?" I asked.

"Since your ex-husband fired him," the man replied.

'Dammit Tony!' I thought as I walked away.

Tony knew I had the hots for Winston, and I was sure that was the reason he fired him.

Being in the old area was nice, so I visited a local bar we used to visit frequently.

"Long time no see," Rebecca said as I sat at the bar.

"Yeah, it's been a while," I nodded.

"Usual?" Rebecca asked.

"You remember?" I asked.

"Coming right up," she smiled.

"Damn," I said, biting into the greasy turkey burger and taking a large slurp of my root beer float.

"Been a while," Rebecca nodded.

"You have no idea," I said, enjoying my favorite burger. Yes, it was greasy and not healthy, but it tasted good.

"I heard about you and the sleaze ball," Rebecca said, sitting on the stool before me.

It wasn't a busy bar, just a hole in the wall Tony and I had found. If you walked or drove too fast, you would go right past it, but the food was good, the drinks were strong, and the music was okay.

"Yeah," I shook my head as the taste of the grease and cheese made me feel like I was ten years younger.

"He still comes in here," Rebecca said.

I nearly choked on my food. I took another swig to clear my throat.

"What!" I exclaimed.

"Brings that bottle blonde with him, and sometimes they come with a few guys, or one guy," Rebecca said.

"And they do what?" I asked.

"Sit in that corner over there," Rebecca pointed to the far corner. "I am telling you, what they do to each other makes my skin crawl."

I looked behind me at the corner stall with the circular bench.

"Like what?" I asked.

"Trust me, you don't want to know," Rebecca shook her head. "You're lucky you got out. The man you married is long gone."

Rebecca got up and waddled over to the next person at the bar.

I looked over at the corner.

"Hey Eliza," I said after eating and paying for my tab.

"Heya," Eliza answered as she picked up the phone.

"I need a favor," I said.

"White person favor," Eliza asked.

"Definitely, who do you know that lives down by the sixteenth bridge?" I asked.

"What are you doing down there?" Eliza asked. "It's getting close to dark."

"Old territory I will fill in you when I get back," I said as I got back in my car.

"A few street girls, some old friends and a really bad ex-boyfriend, take your pick," Eliza responded.

"How bad?" I asked as I started my car.

"If you want someone to disappear for good, bad," Eliza said. "We shouldn't talk on the phone if...."

"Not that one, the friends?" I asked.

"Oh, a few back stabbers, gold diggers and a gossip queen," Eliza said.

"The last one," I nodded. "I will fill you in when I get back."

IT TOOK TWO WEEKS, but Eliza's friend finally came through. She came by the club during off hours.

"We are officially caught up," Eliza's friend said as she pointed at Eliza. "I owe you nothing."

"What you got?" I asked.

"No, first I want her to say it," Eliza's friend said as she held her phone.

"Depends on what you got," Eliza responded.

"Fine," the friend said. "Your ex is fucking nasty, and that's coming from me. I thought I did some freaky shit, but what he and those others do to each other is plain nasty!"

"Tony!" I said, shaking my head as I looked at the photos.

"We are good," Eliza said as the two shook hands.

"Fucking white people," the friend said as she left her phone.

"You want your phone?" I asked.

"I got a new one, keep that one," the friend said. "Don't want it no more!"

I didn't blame her.

"That's your ex-husband?" Eliza asked.

"Yeah," I replied.

The images and videos showed a man I didn't even recognize anymore doing things with other men and women that I couldn't even put into words, and for some of them, I had to turn my head as I didn't want to see them.

"Don't let your kids see this," Eliza said.

"No, never!" I said, reaching over the bar and grabbing the hammer we used to break the heavy ice.

I smashed the phone into pieces. "That book is closed."

"Amen," Eliza nodded.

Chapter Six: Looking Back.

"Holy fuck!" Winston shouted as he came inside me for the third time.

"Damn! You are one hot piece of fucking ass. I tell you!" He gave my large ass a loud smack as his dick fell out of my cum filled hole.

Winston plummeted onto the couch.

"Calling it quits already?" I asked, staring at the sweat rolling down his face and chest.

"I don't know how an idiot like Tony kept up with you," Winston said.

Winston had heard I had been looking for him, and he came by the strip club. We went out for drinks and to grab something to eat, then one thing led to another, and now we had fucked three times in his living room.

"Forgot to say it's a nice house," I said as I finally got to look around.

"It's hers," Winston nodded.

"Bathroom?" I asked.

"Down the hallway to the left," Winston said, trying to catch his breath.

I slowly walked down the hall, looking at pictures of Winston's new wife.

"She looks young," I said.

"Eleven years younger than me," Winston responded.

Skinny too, I thought as I stopped at a picture of her with two young boys.

Never thought Winston would be the type to go after a young woman with kids that weren't his own after his ex-wife Sheila filed for divorce and took their three kids with her.

"They are good boys," Winston said from behind me.

"They look it," I smiled.

"Bathroom," Winston said, opening the door.

The bathroom was nice and clean and smelled fragrant, with small plants in the corners.

I took a quick shower and got dressed.

"So," Winston said as I got out.

"So," I said as I met him in the spacious kitchen of another woman's house.

"You were never here," Winston said, staring at me.

"Where?" I asked.

"Good," Winston smiled.

"You have a good thing going here," I looked at the large backyard through the glass doors.

"Nope," Winston shook his head. "Not telling you."

"Okay," I nodded, getting the hint.

A quick fuck was all he wanted, and I was good with that; I smiled at him as I headed to the front door.

"See you around," Winston said.

"Nope," I replied.

I got what I wanted; he got what he wanted. I had no problems with fucking a married man.

I THOUGHT ABOUT THAT on the drive back home. The old me would have never done that, not in a million years. Marriage was sacred to me back then. I don't know what changed, but I liked it.

A lot had changed since my divorce; for one, I now had two dogs, and I felt bad that Chuck didn't have someone to play with other than myself, so I got another dog to be his friend. The two were inseparable.

The other thing that had changed was my clothes. I usually tried to hide my big features with lengthy jeans or baggy clothes; now, I wore clothes that hugged every inch of my skin. Tight jeans or shorts, and tops that showed off my bust, nothing too over the top but enough to get people's attention.

Tony would hate to go out with me these days. He would hate that I had cleavage showing. I stopped in the bathroom as I caught myself thinking about the old Tony.

"I need to stop that," I told myself in the mirror.

That Tony was gone. The Tony that would beat a man for looking at me twice was gone. The man that would make love to me until we both got what we wanted was gone. The man that gave me my children was gone. The man I saw in those videos wasn't my Tony, and I had a sinking feeling I would never see my Tony again.

I felt a bit sad, not for me or feelings for him. But of him. I felt bad for Tony. Whatever was going on in his head that made him enjoy being treated like that was my fault.

"No!" I shook my head. "He wanted it, not you, he wanted to be treated like that, and you stood your ground," I told myself in the mirror.

My phone rang in the next room.

"Hey," I smiled.

"Just wanted to check on you," Roxxy said.

"A bit of self-pity, but I can handle it," I smiled.

"Good," Roxxy said. "Some of your girlfriends are here, feel like partying?"

"Sure, do," I nodded.

"See you when you get here," Roxxy said.

Another thing that I had gotten used to was hanging out with the girls. I didn't do much of it while I was with Tony as I wanted to spend time with him, but now I loved it.

"You're being checked out," Lauren said, smiling at me as we sat at the bar.

"Who?" I asked.

What guy would be coming to a male strip club and checking out a woman?

"Two of them," Roxxy smiled as she poured us drinks.

"Two?" I asked.

Sure enough, two guys on the other side of the bar waved at me.

"Not too bad," I smiled.

"Probably chubby chasers," Joy remarked.

I knew she meant it as a snide comment, probably to bring me down, but I was having a great night, and she wouldn't rain on my parade.

"I will go and find out," I smiled.

"No way," Lauren smiled as I left their side.

"Hello," I said as I approached the two guys.

"Guess you caught us," one of the guys said. He was attractive in that young man's vibe; the other was older, maybe a friend of a friend.

"So, what are two straight guys doing at a male strip club?" I asked as Roxxy came over. She was tending the bar tonight.

"Well," the older one started. "I am straight he is...."

"Bi," the younger one interrupted.

"Ah," I nodded.

"That answers that," Roxxy smiled.

"It's his birthday and I decided to come along," the older gentleman said. "Roy," he introduced himself.

"Curt," the younger one said.

I introduced myself and Roxxy, and the four of us talked. I liked Roy a lot more than Curt, who was too immature for my liking.

"Fuck them!" Roxxy yelled as Curt fucked her huge tits.

"Yes! Harder!" I yelled as Roy smacked my large ass.

Who knew an older man like Roy had such an appetite for sex? He was fucking me harder than most men half his age.

Another thing added to my list was fucking someone I barely knew. The talk downstairs led to the four of us coming up to Roxxy's office for a private conversation and drinks, which now led to me face down and ass up on the floor, with Roy behind me.

"Harder!" I yelled as Roy smacked my ass again.

My big ass slapped against him as he fucked me hard. The old man looked like a silver fox but had a dick as hard as a rock and knew how to use it.

I looked over at Roxxy, who was lying on her back on her table as young Curt straddled her chest and fucked her fake tits.

Roy pulled on my hair as he emptied his balls inside of me.

"I want a piece of her fat ass," Curt said as he climbed off Roxxy.

"Think you can handle it kid?" I smiled as he got behind me. "It's bigger than most of your college girls."

"You're all talk now," Curt said as he pushed his cock into me.

He was a little longer than his friend, but I was sure he wouldn't last as long.

Roy was fucking Roxxy's mouth as it hung off the table. For an old man that just came inside me, he already had his dick hard and ready to go.

"FUCK YES!" I YELLED the following night.

I never went back into a man's house after a one-night stand. Hell, I never had a one-night stand, but Roy's cock was back inside me for the second night in a row.

There was no Curt or Roxxy, just the two of us this time.

"Fucking take it, you fat bitch!" Roy said with his dick balls deep in my ass.

I had done anal before with Tony, but Roy was the first to conquer my ass. I was again face down on his tiled floor. He had my ass high up and was straddling my ass as he drove his cock into it.

"Yes, call me names," I said as he moved one of his feet to push my head down.

"Shut up!" he yelled, his foot on my head as he fucked my ass hard. "If I wanted my cock sleeve to talk, I would ask it to," Roy shouted down at me. His barefoot on my face pushing down on me as he fucked me hard.

I kept quiet as he used me to get himself off for the second time. He slammed his cock into my ass and came.

"Now, you can get up," Roy ordered.

I got up with a smile on my face.

"Thank you," I smiled.

"I wasn't done with you, I got...." Roy said before I started heading for my clothes on the floor. "Where are you going?" Roy asked.

"Home," I smiled.

"I didn't tell ...." Roy said, but I had already started to put my clothes back on.

I held my hand up. "It was a good time Roy," I nodded. "You have a magnificent cock, and I am sure we will do this again, sometime," I said. "But I have two dogs at home that I need to get back to and well," I shrugged. "You're just a good fuck, I am not looking for anything more."

Roy stood speechless as I started walking to the door. "Call you?" Roy asked.

"We will see," I said as I walked outside.

I already had a dominant male relationship with Tony. And for a nice cock and a good fuck I would probably venture Roy's way again, but it wasn't what I was looking for in a relationship.

I loved my newfound freedom and didn't want some guy thinking because he was a good fuck, he could dominate all of me.

"Hey guys," I said as my two dogs jumped and down as I entered the door.

"Sorry," a voice said from my living room. "I got them all hyped up after our run."

"Who are you?" I asked the stranger in my house.

"Hank's nephew," the tall, dark man said.

"Ah," I smiled. "Hank had told me his nephew Stephen was coming to stay with him for a while."

"Sorry, he didn't tell you I would be watching them," Stephen said.

Hank was getting up there in years, and I was sure it had slipped his mind.

"It's a good thing that you are doing," I said as the two settled down.

"My uncle has been a cornerstone in my life for many years," Stephen said. "It's nothing to make sure he is happy for however long he has left."

"Not many people see their elders that way," I said.

"I better get back over there," Stephen said. "Nice to meet you."

"You too," I smiled as I let him out.

"Wow," I said as I watched Stephen walk across the road to Hank's house. "You got some explaining to do Hank."

"SO, HE'S HOT?" ELIZA asked.

"Hot isn't the word," I said, shaking my head. "Fucking amazing!"

"You saw all that in a few minutes?" Lisa asked.

"He was in my house, in the living room, with the lights on," I said. "Oh yeah, I saw it all."

"Explain again," Eliza said.

"Okay, you know the wrestler, that turned actor?" I said.

"Sweetie there are a lot of those," Lisa said.

"Okay, I think his name is Dwayne something," I said.

"The Rock? You're talking about The Rock?" Eliza shook her head.

"Whatever, I don't pay attention to that stuff," I said. "Imagine his body with Elba's face and skin tone."

"Holy fuck!" Lisa said.

"Yeah, the deep voice too," I said.

"But you said Hank's an old white guy," Eliza said.

"Exactly!" I said.

"And he is this Stephen guy's uncle?" Lisa asked.

"Yes," I said.

"How?" Lisa asked.

"Easy," Eliza shrugged. "Either Hank's brother or sister got with some black person," she said as she got up from the bar.

"But that dark?" I asked.

"It happens," Eliza shrugged. "Come on, you went to medical school you should know some genes are strong than others, probably the black male or female's genes were stronger. It happens a lot."

"I have never seen it, in person," I said.

"Me neither, usually mixed is mixed," Lisa said.

"You have never heard some white man say the kid isn't his because the kid came out a bit darker?" Eliza asked.

"Sure, but usually that's because she cheated," Lisa smiled.

"Stick to dancing and stripping," Eliza shook her head. "No, because not all you white people come from clear cut white families," Eliza said. "You do know that some of your ancestors come from different countries or slept with other races, especially slaves that they *didn't sleep with'* right?"

"So?" I asked. I knew the stories and learned some enslavers slept with their help, especially the male owners.

"As I said, sometimes those genes lay dormant for many generations then come out of the blue and say, *'Hey remember me?'* and bam, a darker child," Eliza said. "And sometimes she did cheat."

"I didn't think about that," I said.

"Not many of you do," Eliza said. "We do. How do you think some of those kids end up for adoption or in the system?"

"Way to put a dampener on things," Lisa said as she sat back down.

"Truth hurts," Eliza shrugged. "I will bet money, if Hank's sister or brother didn't get with a black person, their family lines run through the deep south, or through Europe."

"South," I nodded. "Hank is from Mississippi, originally."

"There you go," Eliza nodded. "It's a hello gene, probably surprised the fuck out of his parents."

"Stephen did say Hank did a lot for him," I said.

"Probably raised him, after they kicked him to the curb or didn't want him," Eliza said. "Like I said it happens a lot!"

I COULDN'T GET WHAT Eliza said out of my head. So, when I came home, I went over to Hank's house.

"Cynthia," Hank said from his chair in the living room.

"Don't get up," I smiled.

The nurse assistant smiled at me as she adjusted his chair.

"What brings you over?" Hank asked. "My nephew did walk your dogs, right?"

"Yes," I smiled.

Hank was dying from a form of cancer. He didn't want to be at some home somewhere. I wouldn't have let him walk my dogs or come over if I had known. It wasn't until all the medical equipment showed up that I found out.

"He is a good kid," Hank said.

"He isn't a kid," the nurse smiled. "He is a grown man."

I smiled at her as she left the room.

"She's the bitter one," Hank whispered. *"I prefer the blonde."*

"Most guys like the blonde ones," I said.

Hank smiled.

"I have to ask something," I said, leaning forward.

"How come Stephen is black?" Hank nodded, wiping his mouth after violently coughing.

"Guess you get asked that a lot," I smiled.

"Since the day he was born," Hank said. "No, none of my family dated blacks or colored as they are called these days. Our families were very strict about mixing the races. Too bad some of their parents didn't feel the same way."

"So, someone down the line?" I asked.

"One of those idiots on my grandfather's side," Hank said. "Knocked up some slave girl and never told anyone."

"Stephen?" I asked.

"Dorothy, my sister was shunned," Hank shook his head. "People called her names everywhere she went and said she cheated on her husband. She never did. That wasn't my Dorothy," Hank shook his hand at me. "She took her own life because of how she was treated and looked at by everyone we knew and loved."

"I am sorry," I said.

"Stephen was the one that found out everything," Hank said. "Bright kid, when he got into high school, he went through all the books and papers and found it all out. Showed everyone up. They were embarrassed, but it was too late for Dorothy. She killed herself when Stephen was seven years old. "

"Sorry to dredge all that up," I said.

"You're a therapist, it's what you do," Hank smiled. "Dredge up the past to find out about the present."

I nodded.

"He's a good kid," Hank said. "Never got angry at anyone, not even when his father came back into his life. Stephen didn't hold a grudge; he welcomed his father with open arms."

"Better than me," I said. "I wouldn't have."

"I didn't, not once did he stand up for Dorothy, he was worse than all the others put together," Hank said. "I haven't talked to that man since Dorothy's funeral. I told him if I ever saw him again, I would kill him. I still mean it."

I smiled, thinking about how feeble Hank looked; trying to hurt a butterfly would take all his energy, let alone a grown man.

"He likes you," Hank smiled.

"Who?" I asked.

"Who else?" Hank smiled. "Sometimes after he gets off work or after a run, he sits right over there peering out the window to see if you are home."

"Get out," I smiled.

"I am serious," Hank said. "I think he has a crush on you."

Stephen was probably a few years younger than me. I knew Hank was many years older than me, probably old enough to be my father.

"Alright, you got to take a bath and get ready for bed," the nurse said as she returned. "Sorry, you've got to go."

"Told you," Hank whispered. *"Mean and bitter!"*

"Be nice," I smiled.

I waved goodbye and then headed out the door.

As I crossed the street, I saw Stephen returning to the house. I waved over at him. He waved back.

'Damn!' I thought, staring at his bulging muscles and those big arms.

If he had a crush on me. I was sure going to take advantage of it.

Chapter Seven: Getting Things Done.

"**H**oly shit," I said as I got off the treadmill.

"You did a lot better today," Stephen said as he handed me a water bottle.

"Tell that to my legs," I responded as my thighs felt like they were on fire.

I didn't know trying to get into a man's pants would be so hard.

I had tried everything, low-cut tops, with my boobs spilling out, telling him my bra size, flirting, and none of it worked.

We were still in the friendship phase. All I wanted him to do was fuck me. Was that so hard?

"If you're serious about toning up, you have to do some cardio," Stephen reiterated.

What finally got him to take notice of me was asking him to help me lose some weight. I had told a little lie that one of my friends was getting married, and I had seen a dress I wanted to wear, but I wanted to lose some weight first. Not a lot, just some.

It wasn't a total lie. One of my friends was getting married, and I had seen a dress I liked; losing weight was a lie. I liked being fluffy or chubby, and I had no intention of losing any weight that would make me lose any amount of boob fat I had; I enjoyed my breasts just the way they were.

Even now, they were gaining attention from other men in the gym, except for the one I wanted.

"So," I said as I caught my breath. "How is Helen?" I asked.

Helen was the lucky woman that got to spread her legs and have this perfect specimen of a man plow her insides.

"She's doing good," Stephen nodded as we walked to the stair machine. Or the machine I had nicknamed the devils' stairs. "Plans to move up here in two weeks."

Hank was getting close to what he was calling the sell-by date. I wasn't looking forward to the news of his passing, but the older man was ready to see his wife, Ellen, so I was trying to be happy for him. I could see Stephen was taking it hard.

It was probably why he wasn't paying me much attention. I had seen the pictures of Helen. She was nothing to look at physically. But Stephen loved her, so who was I to question tastes? After all, the man I married was now a cuck, or even worse, a man slave to one of my ex-friends.

I had to see it for myself, so one night, I went to the bar and saw Tony in person. His eyes lit up when he saw me, but mine dimmed.

He wasn't the man I married, not even close. I had nothing against anyone's kinks or fetishes. I couldn't. I was now a strip club manager, which came with many prejudice and rumors of its own, but seeing what Tony had become was beyond all my thoughts or imagination.

He wanted to talk, hang out, and show me his *friends,* what I called masters. As his girlfriend kissed and hugged three very big and burly or even what I called thuggish guys, the guys called him names that I couldn't repeat even to myself, and Tony loved it.

I pulled Tony aside away from Teresa and her thugs. I looked him in the eyes to see if there was any part of my Tony anywhere deep inside them, but there wasn't he was gone. He loved being this sissified shell of a man more than anything we ever had; he called it feeling like his true self for once.

I warned him there, and then if he ever came near my children like this, I would go to jail a happy woman. I then yanked Teresa out of her table by her hair and told her to keep him away from them as well. Teresa knew me well enough to know it wasn't a threat. I told Tony goodbye that night, and I didn't look back.

Now it was my turn to be happy. For what it was worth, Tony had found his happiness, and even though I and many others disliked the idea of what he had become, he was thrilled with the man he had become.

A huge part of me was happy for him; the other part was disgusted, but it was his life. He could live it the way he wanted.

"I will be back in ten minutes," Stephen said as I started the machine.

"I will be here," I said as I started on the devil's stairs. *Probably dead, but here,'* I thought.

My boobs bounced up and down and garnered the attention of many onlookers. But Stephen didn't even look in my direction.

"MAYBE HANK RAISED HIM a little too white," Tabitha said as she tried on the fourth wedding gown.

Four others were in the seating area as we watched her twirl back and forth in the dress.

"That could be an option," Lauren nodded.

"The dress or the too white?" Michelle asked. "Because that dress doesn't look good."

"Sorry," I agreed as Tabitha turned around to us.

"You don't have the boobs for it sweetie," Judy said. "It makes you look really flat."

"I'm not flat," Tabitha barked as she stepped down from the small runway.

"We know," I smiled.

Tabitha returned to the changing rooms with the four women helping her pick out dresses.

"As a board," Lauren said as she left.

"Shush," I said.

"Boob fairy gives and sometimes it forgets," Michelle smiled.

I grabbed the bottles of wine from the tables. "Enough of that for you three!" I exclaimed.

"Hey!" they said in unison.

"We are here to help her, not bring her down," I said. "She has her husband to do that in a couple of years."

We all laughed. Tabitha was in the glowing period of getting married. I remembered how that felt, picking the dress, venue, seating chart, and everything that went with the hoopla of getting married; it was an exciting time.

"So, what do you think?" Lauren asked.

"About what Tabitha said?" I asked, sitting back in the chair.

"Yes," Lauren nodded.

"I mean, most black guys I know love a women with some curves and a dump truck in the back," Michelle said. "I work with a lot of them."

"You work in corrections, most of them are black," Judy corrected.

"Same thing," Michelle smiled.

I had shown them pictures of Stephen's girlfriend. None of them were impressed.

"Everyone has their tastes," I shrugged. "Look at Tabitha."

I liked Tabitha a lot. She was a few years younger than us; this was her first marriage. She made triple what any of us made in a year. And she had saved herself for marriage, something none of us had done. She was bright, wealthy, and had a bright future.

Tabitha didn't have looks; she was skinny as a beanpole, straight up and down. She had short boyish hair, which I was sure was a turn-off for most guys, and she wore glasses constantly because she was blind as a bat. But yet, this guy was marrying her. He had the looks of an NFL football player, muscles, tall, well-structured, and wealthy, so he wasn't marrying her for money.

Stephen's girlfriend and Tabitha had many things in common; if there were a gallery photo for women to be put into the Plain Jane category, they would be front and center.

"Maybe she's a freak in the bed," I said.

"Now you're grasping," Judy said.

"Really grasping," Lauren added.

"He is a man," Michelle said. "You can be the biggest freak, and if a woman like you shows off and flirts with huge boobs and a large ass in front of your man, chances are he is going to pay attention."

"Right," Judy nodded. "Might not leave or do anything, but he will pay attention."

"And he will comment," Lauren added. "Especially after mentioning your bra size. Hell, I am your best friend and I made a comment."

"I said get a reduction," Judy said as she sipped her glass of wine. "Still think you should."

"Fuck that!" I replied. "Not cutting off my nipples and placing them back on again. Have you seen some of those botch jobs?"

Tabitha came down the walkway towards us.

"No!" we all yelled before she even made it to the runway.

Tabitha sighed and turned around.

IN THE END, TABITHA picked a form-fitting wedding dress that suited her.

But I was still left to my thoughts.

Was I falling for Stephen? I thought all I wanted from him was a roll in the hay, to get fucked, to put my legs to the ceiling or be face down and assed up, but now that I talked with the girls, I was starting to think I wanted more, and the more I thought about it, the more I was convincing myself that I wanted a relationship.

"There you go," Eliza said as she entered my office.

"What?" I asked as I stared at the papers on my desk.

"Doing that white people thing," Eliza said as she sat across from me. "Lay it on me."

"No, there is nothing," I shook my head.

"Okay, how many times has the intercom rang, and how many times have I called you?" Eliza said.

"Shit!" I said as I was supposed to announce the winners of the drawing tonight.

"I did it," Eliza said. "So, what is it that has you staring out into space, like a lost astronaut?"

I knew Eliza; she wouldn't let it go, so I told her.

"So," Eliza said. "The brother is in love with a skinny woman. It happens," she shrugged. "My first husband is currently knocking up a white anorexic looking thing," Eliza said.

"How many babies does he have?" I asked.

"Ten, this one makes eleven," Eliza replied.

"Holy fuck! We need to chop his dick off," I said.

"Hey, go for it, it's not mine anymore," Eliza said. "Plus, you guys don't want women to have abortions anymore, what did you think would happen? People having kids all over the place and laying at home collecting money from welfare and every other thing they can get their hands on."

"Don't say all of us, some of us," I corrected. "So, he's in love?"

"Your friend was right; for most men out there, you can flirt, show a little cleavage, and they will make a comment or try to slide up in you on the down low, but those truly and fully in love will not bat an eye," Eliza said. "Take Duncan, for example."

"The bouncer?" I asked.

"Yes! The bouncer who else?" Eliza exclaimed. "I have been trying to get his attention for years, and he hasn't even given me the time of day."

"That's because you're on your fifth baby daddy, and have six kids," I said, sitting back in my chair.

"What's that got to do with anything?" Eliza asked.

"You are damaged goods sweetie," I smiled. "No one wants to throw their wiener down the hallway at school."

"Hey! My shit is good and tight alright," Eliza said as she stood up.

"I bet there are a few lost ex-boyfriends up there," I smiled. "Trying to get out."

"Shut the fuck up!" Eliza smiled.

"No wonder it sounds like you whistle when you walk," I laughed.

"Bitch!" Eliza laughed as she walked out.

I loved talking to Eliza. It always puts me in a good mood. Maybe she was right; maybe Stephen was in love with his girlfriend, and who was I to try and get in the way of that? I was in love once; I married him and had a great family.

THE DREADED DAY CAME when Hank passed away. It had been a tough few days for all of us. I didn't think I would have these strong feelings for an old grumpy man after only a year of knowing him, but Hank got under your skin quickly.

The day before his passing, while the assistant wasn't looking, Hank wanted me to flash him, so I did, who was I to deny a dying man a quick flash of boobs.

I still think about the look on his face. It made me smile and remember the good times. Stephen was taking it hard, his girlfriend Helen was good at comforting him, and she wasn't as bad as I thought, a quiet country girl, who loved and treasured Stephen, so I backed off no more flirting or trying to charm him. He belonged to her, and she loved him.

"Thanks for everything," Stephen said a few days after the funeral.

"No problem," I nodded. "Heading back to Atlanta?"

Stephen sat down on my couch with a loud plump.

"What's wrong?" I asked.

"Can I tell you something?" Stephen asked.

"You're on my couch, and I used to be a therapist," I shrugged as I got up and closed the door.

No one was home, and the front door was locked, so it was just a force of habit.

"Helen wants to go back, but I have grown used to the city," Stephen said.

"Burgers at four am, huh?" I smiled.

"Not just that, but I don't know why but I feel more of a connection to Hank here, then back in Georgia," Stephen said.

"Because Hank hated his hometown," I replied. "He hated the small time thinking, and well, a lot of things I just can't say."

"Yeah," Stephen nodded.

"Talk to her about it," I smiled. "She seems levelheaded, maybe there is a compromise. There is a small town a few miles from here. It has a small country feel to it. Tony and I used to go there to get away from the city, we took the kids there many times. You guys can move there, you will be an hour and a half from the city, and she can have her country atmosphere."

"That's a good idea," Stephen said. "Thanks Cynthia!"

"That will be three hundred," I said as he stood up.

"That was only three minutes," Stephen smiled.

"Four hundred then," I laughed.

"Thanks," Stephen said as he kissed me on the forehead and left.

"Yup," I nodded. "Friend zone."

"DANIEL," I SMILED AS I saw him enter my nightclub. "*The guys are on the other side of the street, it's mainly females in here,*" I whispered.

"*You're funny,*" he whispered back.

He stood at the bar as I poured a few drinks.

"So, what is it?" I asked.

"Is there somewhere we can talk that's less open?" Daniel asked as he looked around the crowded nightclub.

"It's a nightclub," I shrugged. "It's always open and it's always crowded."

"It's a strip club, don't try to make it sound fancy," Daniel shook his head.

"Yes, but on weeknights we take down the runways and level everything out, and it becomes a nightclub, no stripping," I winked. "My idea," I said. "Brings in a ton of extra money."

"Aren't you the bright one," Daniel said as he pushed a picture across the bar.

"Watch the bar for me," I said to Tina. "Upstairs," I said, pushing the picture back toward him.

We walked upstairs, and I quickly turned on him. "You ever do that again and I will have one of my bouncers beat you so bad no one will recognize you!"

"I told you welcome to the big leagues," Daniel smiled. "Don't take it personally. I didn't when you showed me those pictures," Daniel shrugged as he sat down. "It's business."

"Well, fuck that," I said, shaking my head as I sat down.

"Calm down, you're taking this personal, and it's not, I promise you," Daniel said. "I showed you something you want to vanish, and now you have to ask how it goes away."

I took a deep breath. I couldn't be a hypocrite. I had done the same to him; now it was payback time.

"How?" I asked.

Daniel pushed another picture across the desk toward me. "So?" I asked. "He's running for president this year. What has that got to do with me?"

"He is coming to town next week, for one of his rallies," Daniel said.

"Again, what has that got to do with me?" I asked.

"I want one of your so-called dancers to play nice with him, so we can get it on tape," Daniel smiled as he sat back in his chair.

I was not too fond of his smile.

"No," I said, shaking my head. "I won't play in this cesspool you call politics."

"Oh please," Daniel said, shaking his head. "I love it when you idiots call politics a cesspool or a swamp, or all the other stupid childish names your petty minds can come up with," he laughed at me.

"You do know this is how your officials get elected right?" Daniel asked. "Stupid slogans, and hashtags like *'Let's go fucking Brandon,'* are all thought of weeks before they are announced to the public. We can plant a stupid idiot in the crowd to shout it at the right time and you lemmings just fucking jump."

I stared at him with more hatred than I could ever imagine.

"Oh, *Drain the swamp?* Was thought of months before we put it out there, by an intern, straight out of college and *Lock her up*, weeks before by a passing janitor that just said it and someone thought it was funny, but people lapped it up like mother's milk," Daniel laughed.

"You think *Me too*, was something they just came up on the fly, years for that one. No, but go ahead put that flag up, put that stupid sticker on your truck or car and think you are the smart one. We have manufacturers make those *'come and take our guns stickers,'* for pennies, and they sell for dollars. Newsflash! We know no one is coming for their stupid guns, but as long as we put it in ads and say it come election time, boom! Money in our pockets!"

"And that's why I won't play in your game," I shook my head.

"You still don't get it," Daniel laughed. "You already are, the left hating the right, the right hating the left, the centrists hating both sides, you idiots are playing the game without knowing that you are," Daniel laughed.

"I play golf secretly with my counterpart on the left every other Sunday, I went to his Grandson's birthday party a few weeks ago, but in the media and on television, we yell at each other and call each other names. Guess what? It works; you guys jump when we say jump, yell when we say yell, and both sides get paid!"

Daniel laughed loudly. "It's funny, you think we are the swamp, when you guys have the power to drain it, but you don't, because you keep refilling it."

I knew he was right; I could see it in his eyes.

"So, this is what you are going to do, because well, you have no choice, because all of you gave us this power over you," Daniel leaned forward.

"You're going to hate me, and I really don't care. You're going to sit in that chair for about half an hour, then you are going to walk or drive across the street talk to your friend with the huge fake tits and tell her what I said, she will say I am right, and she will talk to her boss," He smiled at me as he stared me down.

"Then one of those stupid sluts' downstairs is going to play nice with him; we will get our photos and videos, put them online. It will be a big scandal. The left will blow their minds as usual. We will all sit around and play our game and secretly go back and forth on who the new president will be, and voila. Election time, I love it! It's like our Christmas," Daniel nodded as he saw the defeated look in my eyes.

Daniel stood up. "I will leave these pictures here for you," he smiled. "See you next week? It's Leon's birthday," he said as he started to exit. "Nice chatting with you."

I looked at the pictures. One of them was with me and Winston in his house having sex. The photo had a perfect view of me bent over with Winston behind me.

Another was of Tony with his new master's getting spit roasted, as the internet had called that position. Tony wore a French main outfit while the two men did whatever they wanted.

The third was a man sitting beside my Daughter and her newborn in the park on a bench.

The message was clear. If I didn't do what they wanted, they would send those pictures to Winston's wife and the other photographs to my kids.

I didn't want to break up a happy home over a one-time thing, and there was no way in hell I would allow my kids to see their father like that; I had no other option.

Roxxy shook her head. "Sorry to get you into this, but he's right," she nodded.

"Every election?" I asked.

"Cynthia don't do this to yourself," Roxxy shook her head. "If you do you will go down a rabbit hole bigger than you can imagine. I will talk to my boss and see what we can do to get you out of everything, but this," she said, looking down at the candidate's photo. "Is going to happen," she shrugged. "I am sorry."

Roxxy got up from her chair and picked up her phone.

I always heard about scandals and what ifs and the people that controlled everything, but I always thought they were made up by people with silver foil hats and conspiracy theory nut jobs, but it was all real.

I got up, staring at Roxxy like I was in a daze.

I felt like someone had pulled me into the matrix and given me the red pill.

'Welcome to the real world, Cynthia, enjoy your stay,' I thought as I got into my car.

The first thing I saw when driving was a truck with a *'Don't tread on me,'* sticker.

"If you only knew pal," I shook my head. "If you only knew."

Chapter Eight: Reaching the End.

"Fuck," I said as I downed another glass.

"Stop it," Roxxy said, rubbing my back as I watched the events on the television.

The news was on, and they were going over the events that transpired. It happened just like Roxxy said it would.

"I did that," I said, feeling sick to my stomach.

"You did not," Roxxy said, turning the bar stool toward her. "It's the game," she shrugged. "You're a player in it, now," she smiled. "That's all. You lost this round. Now what are you going to do about it?"

"I want to smash Daniel's head!" I said, slamming the glass down on the table.

"Well, that's violent, and while sometimes it is part of the game. You are too close to him, you know his wife and his kids," Roxxy nodded. "The splash back will hurt you more than him."

"Okay," I relaxed as I turned the television off. "So, what can I do about it?"

"There's my girl," Roxxy smiled. "Like I said it's a game, with stakes involved," she reached into one of her cabinets and pulled out a red and blue folder. "You said you took the red pill now how far into the matrix do you want to go, Neo?"

"All the way," I smiled as I took the red folder.

"YOU FUCKING BITCH!" Daniel yelled at me.

"Business not personal," I smiled.

"No, this is very personal!" he yelled at the back of his house.

I waved inside at his wife, Debra, baking cookies; she smiled at me. "I love her cookies," I smiled.

"Cynthia, this can cost me my job, my retirement, my house. my marriage!" Daniel said.

"Is she making the oatmeal ones, they are really good," I said, pushing him out of the way and looking into the large kitchen.

"Cynthia!" Daniel yelled.

"Daniel, I told you I am the messenger," I shrugged. "Granted I liked being the one to bring it to you, but this comes from Roxxy's boss, whoever he or she is," I said.

Daniel looked inside the red folder. "How did they get all of this?"

"All I was told was that you have four days, to make things right, or all of that goes public," I smiled as Debra and their two sons started putting cookie sheets in the large oven. "How much does a house like this cost?"

"A lot," Daniel said as we stood on the large back porch overlooking an immense backyard. "Upkeep will kill you," he sighed as he put the folder on the round table. "I can't make this right, not in four days, not even in four years. It goes way past anything I can do."

"Then, you better go in there and tell her," I sighed.

"Well played," Daniel nodded. "Hope you're happy?"

"Yup," I nodded. "Very."

I waved at Debra and the kids as I walked around the large building to my car. Roxxy was in the passenger seat.

"Well?" Roxxy asked as I went inside.

"Thank you!" I smiled. "Two families?"

"Yup," Roxxy nodded. "How he did it and kept both a secret I would never know," Roxxy smiled as we pulled away.

"Two, I had trouble with one," I shook my head. "Politicians."

As we drove, Roxxy told me she wanted me to meet someone.

"HERE?" I ASKED. WE were far from the city, and I didn't even know a place like this existed.

"Yup," Roxxy said as we got out and headed into what looked like an abandoned gas station, the ones you saw in old television shows and movies.

The place looked like it hadn't been used while I was alive.

"Are you sure?" I asked, looking at the old rusted gas pumps.

"Definitely," Roxxy smiled.

Empty glass bottles and fast-food containers littered the floor. Many homeless people were in the corner as we entered the building.

"Just passing through," Roxxy said as they looked our way.

The smell of urine and other odors made me put my hand over my nose.

"Roxxy," I said as I walked faster to catch up to her.

"It's okay," Roxxy smiled.

She opened the back-office door and walked inside.

"Sit," she said, pointing to the old desk with old chairs. "Trust me," she smiled.

I sat down, and Roxxy waved. "See you in a bit," she said, hitting the light switch.

The seat and the desk started going down.

"No fucking way," I said as I descended an elevator shaft.

"Yeah, I said the same thing," a white man said.

He was of average build and had mouse-brown hair. "Tony," he said, introducing himself.

"What is this?" I asked as I got up and walked into what looked like an office building.

People were typing away at keyboards and looking at large monitors behind desks. Other rooms were where people were talking and having meetings.

"Well, to make it simple," Tony smiled. "Operations for the East coast."

"Yeah, right," I smiled.

"I said the same thing, two years ago," Tony smiled as we entered a small meeting room. "The truth and scope of all of this will blow your mind," he smiled. "But I am very serious. The entire operation for the East Coast goes through here and one other place just like it. In New York that's where I am from."

"You came to Richmond Virginia, from New York?" I asked.

"Yes," Tony said as he sat down across from me.

"To see me?" I asked.

"Yes, well Roxxy said you were ready, so I had to come see for myself, before you see the others," Tony said. "It's a hierarchy and when the time comes, you will be in this chair talking to someone on that side," he smiled.

"Hierarchy? Like a monarchy?" I asked.

"Now you're getting it," Tony smiled.

"Okay, so why am I here?" I asked.

"Roxxy is getting a promotion, and you're going to take her place, with me helping you," Tony said.

"You're her boss?" I asked.

"No, I am just here to meet and guide you," Tony said. "I have my own area to run, these people are yours, everyone in here will help you."

"So, I am there boss?" I asked.

"No, they will help you, get what we needed done," Tony smiled. "Here, let me start from the beginning."

"That would be great," I nodded.

I SLOWLY WALKED TO the car. Roxxy smiled as I got in the passenger seat.

"Holy fucking crap!" I said as I sat down.

"You need a drink," Roxxy said.

"Holy fucking crap!" I repeated.

"Maybe two drinks," Roxxy laughed.

Roxxy closed both clubs, and we sat in my office as I drank from my glass.

I stared at Roxxy and Eliza.

"You both knew?" I asked.

"Uh huh," Eliza nodded.

Roxxy smiled at me.

"That friend that got the info for me, wasn't a friend?" I asked.

"Nope," Eliza nodded.

"No," Roxxy said as I tried to stand up. "You will faint again."

"Not picking your big ass up again," Eliza shook her head.

"Holy fucking crap!" I said as my mind tried to wrap itself around everything.

"You sure she can handle it?" Eliza asked.

"How did you fair when you heard?" Roxxy asked.

"I drank, fucked a few guys and then I accepted it," Eliza said. "She looks paler than usual, and that's saying something."

"She will be fine," Roxxy said.

"So," I said, putting the glass down. "There is a Monarchy of sorts, and they rule everything, every city, every country, everything?"

"Yup," Roxxy nodded.

"In a nutshell," Eliza responded.

"Secret societies were real, but now they are dying out because they," I said, shaking my head. "Used to much of the tree of life potion or some shit?"

"Yup," Roxxy smiled. "Told you she is getting it."

"I will run operations for the whole state of Virginia?" I asked.

"Yes, with Eliza," Roxxy smiled.

"Out of a strip club?" I asked.

"Batman has the bat cave?" Eliza smiled.

"Okay," I shrugged. "Think I got it."

"You do?" Eliza asked.

"Fuck no!" I shouted. "Are you insane?"

"Told you," Eliza shook her head.

"Okay, calm down, it's a lot to grasp, but think about it rationally," Roxxy said.

"I did, the fourth time he tried to show me, and the videos and the papers, and the recordings, and the...." I said.

"She's going to faint again," Eliza said.

"AGAIN?" I ASKED AS I sat up on my couch in the office.

"Yup," Roxxy smiled at me.

"Sorry," I smiled back.

This time it was just her.

"Happens," Roxxy shrugged.

"I need Lauren," I nodded. "If I am going to do this, and I want to do this, but I need someone I can count on."

"Understood," Roxxy smiled. "I can arrange that, anything else?"

"The criminal stuff?" I asked. "That's a given?"

"Welcome to the crime world," Roxxy shrugged. "Can't have a perfect world without it, ying and yang and all that stuff."

"Okay, Eliza can handle that part," I nodded as I sat up.

"Agreed," Roxxy said. "So? What do I tell them?"

"I'm in," I shrugged. "What the hell?"

There is always a moment of clarity in knowing things are out of your control and within it.

I started feeling secure as I drove home, knowing I was part of something much larger than most people could imagine. I asked Tony why everything wasn't made public, but then before he answered, I knew the answer.

Most Americans couldn't handle the results of election results without flying off the handle or court results without rioting.

Hell, even the outcome of a sports game had a city in fear. Knowing what I knew now would have people in disbelief, suicidal, and in the end, anarchy. Even religion itself would fall apart.

My father once said the entity of God itself could come down to Earth and make itself known, and the truest of believers would still say it didn't exist.

If that entity told humans what they were doing was wrong, what they thought about the bible was wrong, and tried to make things right, humans would try to kill it.

Humans, as a whole, aren't ready or will never be prepared for the unknown. It is why we are both scared and curious about the dark or space, we want to believe we are ready, but at the same time, we are afraid of what happens if we do.

As much television or movies lead us to believe that we would one day become one planet and form a harmonious civilization, that was all make-believe.

Humans like to be able to point the finger at someone else and say, *'You're the reason my life is bad, or you're making things worse,'* not one of us is ready to say we are the reason for our own faults and our own problems. Until that day comes, we aren't prepared for the truths of the past or the future.

"Of course," Lauren said as I brought her into the loop.

"What?" I asked as she stared back at me. "You're not going to freak out, or go crazy or faint?"

"Why would I?" Lauren shrugged. "I am not small minded enough to think that there isn't a larger scheme to everything."

"Just like that?" I asked.

"Yup," Lauren said as she sipped on her wine.

I shook my head.

"You freaked out, didn't you?" Lauren smiled.

"Fainted twice," I smiled.

We both laughed, and I was glad to have my best friend on my new adventure.

MONTHS PASSED, AND I had to say being a crime lord and a governing body simultaneously suited me. I wouldn't say I was getting excited every day at work, but having the ability to make an actual change when I wanted was becoming something I looked forward to daily.

"They are at it again," I said, entering my office. "I see one more article about those idiots on the news I swear I will level that whole area."

"On it," Eliza said. "What do you want a sting or a bust?"

"Bust, I like the mayor," I smiled. "Make it seem like it was his idea."

"Good idea," Lauren nodded.

"Just don't make him go on one of those long ass rants, short and sweet," I said, sitting down.

I loved moving things around on the giant chessboard that had become my state. Sometimes things went my way, and I loved it; other times, I was told to tone it down, which was fair.

"Oh no," I said, looking at the video of my house. "He's back."

"Go, we got this," Lauren smiled.

The one thing that hadn't changed was my feelings for Stephen.

"Hey," I said as I came home and saw him sitting on my stairs.

"Hey," he smiled back at me.

"Didn't work out, huh?" I asked.

"We are having problems again," Stephen said as I opened the door.

"Thought so," I nodded.

With my new activities, part of me wanted to do immoral things, like get involved with my personal life. Help my children, get Frederick out of the military or stuff like that, but I didn't, they were grown adults, and while their mom was now someone that could make their lives a lot better, it was up to them if they wanted me to, and so far, they showed no signs.

I had told them everything, and at first, they laughed except Frederick, who said he guessed things like that were happening.

It took a few weeks, but they decided they wanted no part of it. So, they were on their own.

I still played mother hen and kept an eye on things. I gave a little nudge to get Dawson the promotion he wanted, nothing significant that would show I helped, but enough to get the job done.

I also helped Mike and Katy get the house they wanted, but I saw that as small things.

"Well, there's the couch," I smiled.

"No, just came over for a drink really," Stephen said.

"That I can do," I smiled.

If Stephen only knew that people were around my house right now looking after my security, he might not be so relaxed. Like at the gas station, the homeless people were security agents.

The person walking the dog, the guy across the street watering his flower bed, and the young girl running laps were all part of my security team.

"So, what are you going to do?" I asked.

"I haven't sold my uncle's house, I thought about moving in," Stephen said. "Helen wants us to take a break, to sort things out."

"That would be nice," I smiled.

"Can I ask you a personal question?" Stephen said, leaning forward.

"Absolutely," I smiled.

"Does size matter?" he asked.

I nearly coughed on my wine as I slowly regained my composure.

"I have been asked that many times," I said as I looked at him. "Both professionally and personally, and I always answer the same, depends on the person and the level of intimacy."

"Okay," Stephen nodded.

"Why what happened?" I asked.

"She says I am too big, well too thick her words not mine," Stephen said.

"Can happen," I nodded.

"Plus, she doesn't like it when I ejaculate," Stephen said.

"Cum, I hate using the word ejaculate," I shook my head. "Why not?"

"It's messy," Stephen said.

I laughed as he said, "That's half the fun," I smiled. "Does she spit it out or swallow?"

"Neither, she has never done that," Stephen shook his head.

"Oh, wow," I smiled. "You poor poor man," I said.

"I got used to it," Stephen said. "We have been together since high school."

"Wait?" I said, putting my glass down. "So, you have never had a woman suck your cock?"

"No," Stephen said.

"Well, that's," I said as I stopped myself from being rude.

"I know crazy," Stephen said, drinking his beer.

"Sad, very sad," I corrected. "You ever wanted her to?"

"Oh yes," Stephen said. "She said it's messy and not right."

A smile crept over my face as I saw the look in his eyes as he looked at me.

"Do you want me to?" I asked, knowing the answer.

"I mean, I couldn't," Stephen stuttered. "It wouldn't be..."

"Now," I said, moving around the small marble counter in my kitchen. "I am not like your girlfriend," I said as Stephen looked at my body. "I am much bigger," I moved my hands over my colossal chest, thick waist, and hips. "Are you sure?"

The look on Stephen's face as my hands massaged my chest told me all I needed to know. I pressed the small device in my palm that signaled my secret protection personnel to leave me alone.

"Sit," I smiled as I took his hand and led him to the couch.

I knelt in front of him as I saw the look of anticipation in his eyes.

"It's pretty big," Stephen said.

"I am a big girl," I smiled at him. "I can handle it."

Most men thought their cocks were big or thick. Especially most black men. Vince was the only black man I knew with a massive cock, and I was sure Stephen wasn't even close to being that big.

"Well," I said. I even surprised myself as I took out Stephen's cock.

It wasn't massive, but it was pretty thick and long, I would guess just a bit longer than eight inches.

"I told...." Stephen started to say before I took his cock into my mouth.

I loved the utter look of disbelief he had on his face as I downed his entire cock, feeling its length pass through my lips and into my throat. I angled my approach to ensure it went further down my throat, then slowly snaked it back out.

I didn't take my eyes off Stephen as I licked all around his cock.

"That felt good," Stephen said.

"I haven't even started yet," I smiled as I sucked the head before doing what I do best.

Within moments my head was bouncing up and down in his lap. His engorged cock filled my mouth and throat each time I downed my head.

As polite as Stephen was, his natural instincts took over, and he held the back of my head as he pushed my head down onto his cock.

I gasped a little as saliva coated his dick.

"I bet I could do something else she never could," I smiled as I removed my shirt.

Stephen watched in amazement as I took off my bra and let my enormous breasts fall naturally.

"My god!" Stephen exclaimed as my enormous breasts smacked around his cock.

"Told you!" I smiled as I started bouncing my breasts up and down the shaft of his cock.

'I bet he never goes back to her flat chested ass, again,' I thought as he looked down at my massive breasts making his cock disappear.

"Fuck!" Stephen said, as I was sure he had never been tit fucked before.

"I am going to show you things she wouldn't even dream about doing," I said as I looked at him.

"SO, THAT'S HIM?" ELIZA asked as she watched Stephen enjoying himself.

We watched from my office through the one-way glass. Stephen looked like a man who had never been to a strip club before. He watched the women dancing and stripping like a lost puppy.

"You sure you want him down there?" Lauren asked. "With all those other women?"

"Absolutely," I said as I looked at him.

Stephen was mine now. I had shown him a whole new world when it came to sex. Before me, he was like a virgin; now, he had done nearly everything.

I popped his cherry, and he was genuinely grateful for that.

I walked back to my desk.

"You going to tell him?" Lauren asked as she joined me.

"About all this?" I shook my head. "One day, maybe."

"I wouldn't," Eliza said. "He seems goodie two shoes. Might do something stupid."

"The reason why I brought him," I said, looking over some papers.

Being in charge had its benefits, and I have to say the power was growing on me. I wanted to share this world with Stephen, but first, I had to break him from the polite and safe world he had grown accustomed to.

"Actually," I smiled. "Tell Becky and Vanessa to show him a good time."

"How good of a time are we talking?" Eliza asked.

"A very good time," I smiled.

"What are you doing?" Lauren asked as Eliza walked out of the office.

"I need to know if he learned anything from our endeavors," I said, sitting back and watching the video of the private rooms.

I watched Becky and Vanessa take him into the room. Stephen was all hands as he pawed at Vanessa's huge fake tits.

Becky bounced her head on his cock.

"Impressive," Lauren nodded. "Not as big as Vince's but I am impressed."

I turned the volume up and heard everything.

"Fuck me," Vanessa said as she lay on the oversized couch.

Stephen got between her legs and fucked her.

"How far are you going to let this go?" Lauren asked.

"Until I get bored," I smiled.

"So, a long time," Lauren said. "I will go find some fun for myself."

"I heard Mitch has a nice one," I said.

"Might take you up on that," Lauren winked.

I left the video on as I did some work. When Stephen finished with Becky and Vanessa, I sent another two in and another after that, and by the end of the night, my poor Stephen was exhausted.

"Well," I said, entering the private room. "Had enough?"

"No," Stephen said as he pulled me toward him. "They were just a warmup."

"Oh really," I smiled.

The innocent Stephen I knew was gone; he had lust in his eyes and a new hunger for sex and all its perverse pleasures.

Quickly he spun me around.

"It's much bigger than all the others," I said as Stephen bent me over.

"I can handle it," Stephen said as he lifted my skirt and pushed his cock into me with one long thrust.

I felt his thick cock push deep into me; his hand gripped my thick thighs.

"Show me," I said, slamming back onto his cock. "Show me you can handle me."

My large ass slammed back onto Stephen as we fucked in the private room.

They say power corrupts; for a long time, I said it only corrupted those that wanted to be corrupted. Looking at the lust in Stephen's eyes, I knew it corrupted everyone.

"Fuck me!" I yelled. "Fuck me like you would never fuck her!"

Poor Helen had run back to her hometown. Stephen dumped her the day after we fucked; to him, she was nothing compared to me. Her body was unlike mine, and her idea of sex was innocent and pure compared to my depravity.

"Come on!" I said, slamming back onto him. "Fuck my fat ass!"

"I want to," Stephen said.

"Then do it," I smiled.

Stephen took his cock from my pussy and pushed it into my ass.

Another thing Helen would never do, she would never allow Stephen to fuck her ass, but I let him do it on our first night together.

"Like that? You fucking whore!" Stephen yelled with his dick balls deep in my ass.

There was my Stephen, just like they had corrupted me; I was now corrupting those around me. A smile crept over my face as I felt his thick cock fuck my ass.

"Stephen?" I asked. "How do you feel about mountains?"

"What?" he asked.

"Nothing," I said, shaking my head.

He wasn't ready yet, but soon I will bring him into the fold. And he will join me on my new adventure, but for now, he will be my new toy.

The End

Also by Alexander Martin

Office Relations
Office Relations: The New Boss
Office Relations: Helpful Boss

Standalone
A Better View
A Different Kind Of Summer
A Dish Served Cold
A New Direction

About the Publisher

Alexander Martin is the pen name of my Erotic Stories. I love writing. My Erotic Stories dive into my wild side. Most of the stories that you will find under my pen name involve interracial relationships and the pros and cons of being interracial.

Read more at https://medium.com/@alexander-martin/lists.